Amáne of Teravinea

Black Castle

D. María Trimble

Copyright © 2015 D. María Trimble

All rights reserved.

ISBN-10:0985575352
ISBN-13:978-0-9855753-5-9

To unconditional love...

Contents

Chapter One	1	Chapter Seventeen	116
Chapter Two	3	Chapter Eighteen	120
Chapter Three	11	Chapter Nineteen	124
Chapter Four	14	Chapter Twenty	130
Chapter Five	23	Chapter Twenty-one	139
Chapter Six	27	Chapter Twenty-two	143
Chapter Seven	46	Chapter Twenty-three	149
Chapter Eight	52	Chapter Twenty-four	156
Chapter Nine	56	Chapter Twenty-five	162
Chapter Ten	60	Chapter Twenty-six	166
Chapter Eleven	66	Chapter Twenty-seven	176
Chapter Twelve	77	Chapter Twenty-eight	189
Chapter Thirteen	93	Chapter Twenty-nine	205
Chapter Fourteen	101	Chapter Thirty	209
Chapter Fifteen	106	Chapter Thirty-one	211
Chapter Sixteen	112	Chapter Thirty-two	222

"My heart, my love, my Amáne, I kneel before you to make a pledge for all to witness. I promise to always defend you, to honor our union, and love you more each day than I did the day before. I will trust you and respect you; laugh and dance with you when you are joyful; share your tears with you when you are sorrowful. You will always be the color in my day, the salt of my sustenance, until the day I meet my ancestors."

~ Ansel's pledge to Amáne • *The Royal Wedding*

"Ansel, my love and my life, I kneel before you to make a pledge for all to witness. I promise to love you unconditionally, to respect you, to care for and protect you, to comfort and encourage you. In you I have found a great treasure, a faithful friend, my sturdy shelter. Your friendship and love is beyond price. Where you go I will go, where you stay I will stay. You are my heart and my love until the day I meet my ancestors."

~ Amáne's pledge to Ansel • *The Royal Wedding*

Chapter One

Consciousness slowly dawned. I begged it to release me — to let me go back to the darkness that would numb my pain. I lay in a fetal position on a damp floor. A raging fury spiraled in my head. Ringing filled my ears. Words echoed off the walls of my mind. A hot spasm of pain shot up my left arm from the tip of my hand. I clutched at its source, my little finger. A section up to the first joint was missing. My stomach twisted.

What happened? I groaned in agony.

I squeezed my eyes shut and fought the torment that crashed through my body. Pain cried out from every one of my bones.

I needed to awaken from the nightmare.

It has to be a nightmare, this can't be real. Thunder exploded in my skull. A burning feeling rose in my throat.

It's not a dream.

Lifting my hand to the back of my throbbing head, I felt a matted sticky mess. A detached voice called out. But there was no one in here with me. The vocalization was in my head. Pressing my fists into my temples, I tried to silence it.

If I open my eyes, maybe I could find relief.

Blinking several times, I willed my eyes to reveal my surroundings. All that registered was a deep darkness.

Have I gone blind?

Smells of rot and decay assaulted my nose. The heat and humidity added to the difficulty of breathing.

Rolling onto my knees, I struggled to my feet. Sweat soaked my clothing. My hands pushed against a dirt wall. Determined my legs would obey, I grunted as I searched for a grip to steady myself. My muscles trembled in protest. Nausea overcame me, my head spun. I leaned over and vomited, which brought additional shooting pains.

Turning my back to the wall, I let myself slide down to a sitting position.

Where am I?

Voices, or perhaps just one voice, resonated as if in answer to my silent question.

Maybe I've gone mad.

I stretched my feet out in front me, but they hit a stop before my legs could straighten. My lips pressed together. Painfully, I tried again to rise to a standing position. Tottering, I remained on my feet and explored my surroundings. My prison, I discovered, was a round pit, narrower than my extended arms. An oubliette. I'd heard of this ultimate secret dungeon, one in which a prisoner was tossed and forgotten. Looking up cemented my fears. A trapdoor far above let in a sliver of light. I retched again.

"Leave me alone," I whispered as I pulled my hair. The voice wouldn't go away. A cacophony of noises filled my tortured mind.

I sank back down to a curled-up position and let the darkness, like a blanket, fall over me.

CHAPTER TWO

Six days earlier...

"Ow!" I said. "You just stabbed me with that pin." I turned to glare at my friend, Fiona.

A musical laugh escaped her lips. "Well, if you would stop fidgeting, Amáne, I could do my job. Your wedding is only three days away and I still don't have your dress perfect."

"I thought it was perfect when I tried it on weeks ago. You just keep making it tighter. I won't be able to take a full breath. Between lack of air and the terror of being in front of the entire kingdom, you'll have me fainting in a heap at Ansel's feet. If that happens, I will make you regret it."

Fiona laughed again. I rolled my eyes and let out an exasperated sigh. She stopped tugging at my dress and gave me a sideways glance.

My shoulders slumped. "I'm sorry, Fiona. I know I've been hard on you the last few days."

"Last few days? I believe it's more like the last few months."

"Truthfully, Fiona, I know I wouldn't have survived my new duties if you and Kail hadn't agreed to relocate here, so far from home. I'll never be able to repay you."

"Amáne, I believe it is I who owe you. Do you know how long I've set my heart on just visiting this city? The City of Teravinea has been in my dreams all my life. And now Kail and I are actually living here."

Fiona put down her packet of pins and took my hands in hers. "I can't help but shake my head about how our lives have been woven together. Two girls, complete opposites, living in Dorsal, the farthest corner of the kingdom. You were always so private; so much of a loner; so fascinated with swords and knives. You weren't the slightest bit interested in anything feminine."

I smiled. "And all you cared about was ribbons and silk fabric; and who should be marrying whom; and of course all the handsome merchants in the marketplace. That is, until Kail made eyes at you. But you were always so nice to me. I never understood that."

"I thought behind your rebellious façade, you were someone who could be a trusted friend. My mother admired your mother and had always marveled at her selflessness. She told me she thought you were a lot like her, only you hid it for some reason."

I shrugged. "I guess I was just used to keeping to myself."

"And now look at us," Fiona said. "The two of us, good friends, so far from home."

I nodded.

Fiona brightened. "Amáne, I am so happy that you finally found your prince. Literally." She laughed. "Do you know what an epic vows ceremony this will be? Two dragon riders. One, a king, marrying the other, a commoner from Dorsal. King and Queen dragon riders. Never in our long history has there been a story like this." She actually bounced with excitement.

"Please, Fiona, stop. I'm having a hard enough time anticipating the ceremony. Being the center of attention makes me nauseous.

Black Castle

The walls of this castle already feel too confining. I don't know if I can ever mold to the life of a royal."

"Wait until you hear some of the ballads the musicians are practicing for your celebration. Your quests, your accomplishments, are astonishing. They've put them to song magnificently."

"Ugh, are you even listening to me? You're not making this any easier."

"I'm sorry, Amáne. I guess I'm quite nervous, myself. I know my name will never be in ballads, but the success of this monumental undertaking is on my shoulders."

I laughed and wrapped her in a firm hug, hoping the pins in my gown would hold.

Fiona pulled away and tugged me toward the couch. "Amáne, come sit down with me. Let's forget all this for a bit. Do you know what I've been dying to hear from you?"

I shook my head.

"You've never told me of your linking with Eshshah."

"You, Fiona, are interested in my linking story? And now? When you're in the middle of trying to suffocate me with this gown?"

"I'm not all about ribbons and silks. I've been fascinated with stories of dragons since I was little. You and I grew up with the teaching that they were just stories, nothing more. But now," she swept her hand through the air, "it's as if all the myths of Teravinea have jumped out of childrens' fantasy books. Dragons are real! I want to hear, first hand, about Eshshah's hatching. The ballads just aren't enough for me."

I beamed. There was nothing a dragon rider liked to talk about more than his or her dragon.

"Very well, then, I'd love to tell you. And mind you, I've only told the whole story to the Healer and Ansel. I don't know what the ballads say, but they could only fall short."

I started to take a deep breath, but she had me pinned so tightly in my gown. I scowled and fidgeted. Fiona ignored my discomfort. She gestured impatiently for me to start.

I took a medium-size breath and began, "The day after Mother passed to her ancestors, I made the decision about where I'd go for my memorial journey. To honor her memory, I decided to hike to our cove. You know, where she and I always went to get away for a few days?" Fiona nodded. "Mother and I loved camping there. It was our private time together."

"Why did you decide to go alone? Weren't you afraid? I would imagine the Healer or Gallen would have felt it a privilege to accompany you."

I shrugged. "I wasn't afraid. At least not at first. I just wanted to be by myself, so I packed and left without thinking too much about it. It took me a couple hours to hike to the cove. Then I set up my camp, just the way Mother and I used to. I had to rebuild our fire ring, so I searched for some large rocks nearby.

"Later, as I sat by my campfire, I sang some grieving songs. That's when I regretted my hasty decision to go off on my own. I wasn't as fearless as I'd thought. Mother had told me whenever I got frightened, I should sing so she could hear me. So, I chose my favorite ballad about an ancient battle and sang it loud."

Fiona leaned in.

"The more frightened I got, the louder I sang. Then, I heard a humming sound, like someone accompanied my song. The sound came from one of the rocks that made up my fire ring."

"But it wasn't a rock. It was Eshshah's egg," Fiona blurted out.

"Yes." I smiled. "I couldn't keep my eyes off the egg when it started vibrating. I felt compelled to put my hands on the shell. It shook harder as cracks formed along the top. A red glow seeped

BLACK CASTLE

out of the fissures, like a flame burned inside. The egg split open. Eshshah fell out. So tiny. Her scales glowed like she was on fire. Like a hearth fire." I closed my eyes. It was as if I was there again at her hatching. "She was the most beautiful thing I'd ever seen."

"Amáne?"

I gave Fiona a sheepish look. "I'm sorry, Fiona. I guess I got a little distracted. What did you ask?"

Fiona's face glowed with emotion. "I wanted to know how big Eshshah was."

"Not much bigger than one of your aunt's barn cats."

"I always thought those were big cats," she said. "But when I think of Eshshah that small, it's hard to believe. Please go on."

"Well, as I stared at the radiant little dragon, I was drawn into her whirling golden eyes. As soon as she had me mesmerized, she pulled back her head and struck me with her fangs." I grabbed my shoulder, closing my hand over the linking mark.

Fiona jerked her head back, concern written on her face.

I continued, "She inadvertently injected her full measure of venom. The pain was excruciating. My dragon fever lasted three days and nearly sent me to my ancestors." I swallowed. "Fiona, I saw my mother."

"Your mother?" Fiona's face went white. "On the Other Side?"

I shook my head. "The Shadows."

Her mouth fell open. She exhaled a quick short breath.

"If it weren't for Eshshah's extraordinary healing powers, I wouldn't be here, today. Eshshah probably wouldn't either."

Fiona blinked back her tears and squeezed my hand. "I'm thankful for her powers."

Her eyebrows drew together in a puzzled frown. "Since we knew nothing of dragons and linking, you must have been terrified all alone, not knowing what to expect. But what about all the other dragon riders who knew the linking ritual? I don't understand. How would they ever volunteer to participate in a hatching, knowing they would go through such intense suffering?"

I laughed. "Fiona, doesn't every woman know there's pain and possible death from childbirth? And yet, still we accept it for the miracle of having a baby in our arms."

With a wistful look, Fiona said, "You're right, I never thought about that."

Fiona paused before she asked, "So, Eshshah's bite is what created your linking mark on your shoulder?"

"Yes, it's a representation of her, and it's our seal that we're forever linked."

Fiona giggled. "I thought it was a tattoo that all dragon riders had to get. What happened next?"

"Once I came out of my dragon fever, Eshshah and I spent time getting to know each other. It was an uncommon linking. We were on our own and had to teach each other what most dragon riders learned from their superiors and peers. She explained that we could speak to each other without using our voices — thought transference. At first we were afraid to reveal ourselves. Eventually, we told the Healer, and that's when Eshshah and I went to live with her."

I threw up my hands. "That's the story of our linking."

The smile still on her face, Fiona said, "Thank you, Amáne. I've always wanted to hear that story from you. May I have your permission to tell it to Rio and Mila? My silly sisters do nothing but talk about being dragon riders. They are so much not like me." Her sweet-sounding laugh filled the room.

I nodded. "Of course you can tell them."

"They've been so excited seeing all the dragons flying in and out of the city transporting your guests."

Black Castle

"The Ancient Ones, from the Valley of Dragons." I said. "Without their help we wouldn't have had the winning advantage in the War of the Crown. I'm still reeling from the fact that so many of them chose to stay."

"All the riders who'd lost their dragons can ride again. It must mean so much to them," Fiona said.

"You have no idea. It's like their lives have been renewed."

At that moment, my beautiful fiery dragon conveyed a message through thought transference. "Amáne, King Ansel and Sovann have just flown in."

I felt her excitement of seeing her mate, the impressive golden dragon, Sovann.

"Hurry," I said to Fiona, "get this dress off of me so I can go see Ansel. They've just flown in."

"Good try, Amáne. Your wedding is in three days. You know the betrothed are not to see each other for the three days before the wedding."

"You can't do this to me, Fiona! He's been away, dealing with the state of affairs in the kingdom. That'll make it six days before the wedding that we won't have seen each other."

Fiona shrugged. "It's been a tradition for countless generations. I had nothing to do with its inception and I will not take any part in breaking it. It's bad luck."

"Bad luck?" I scoffed. "Who would think up such a ridiculous tradition and then brand it bad luck for breaking it? When I'm queen, I guarantee that practice will end. Immediately."

"Well, you're not queen yet. The tradition stands, and it's my duty to make sure you abide by it."

"That's not fair. There should be a special circumstance for Ansel and me."

I felt Eshshah let out a rumble, her version of a laugh.

"Not you too, Eshshah. Don't flaunt the fact this stinking tradition doesn't include dragons. You get to go hunt with Sovann. No one's keeping you two apart."

"Sovann said to tell you King Ansel sends his love. And he longs to see you." Eshshah said before she exited our thought transference.

I huffed in disappointment. My brow furrowed as I jerked my head toward Fiona. "I'm going to let you be the one to tell Ansel he can't see me."

Her eyes went wide.

"And," I continued, "since you've already put me in a foul mood, I need to ask you why you aren't telling me what you have planned? I don't even know the schedule of events. It is my wedding, you know."

Fiona held my shoulders and put her face in front of mine. "I'm sparing you additional stress. I'll let you know the events when you need to know. You asked me to direct your vows ceremony and celebration. Now trust me to do my job." Her expression was firm and unyielding.

"Furthermore," she said, "you're lucky I convinced King Ansel to have his coronation ceremony last month and not combine it with your wedding day. Can you imagine adding that load to your already-full day?"

I shook my head. "I would never have survived."

My expression softened as I held Fiona's eyes. "Forgive my ill-temper, Fiona. I appreciate all you're doing for us, and I don't doubt that it will be the most magnificent, unforgettable, most-talked-about day ever. I do thank you sincerely."

Chapter Three

I sat in my chambers sulking after Fiona left. Surveying my plush surroundings, I couldn't help feeling a pang of guilt for my ill humor. I now lived in the royal wing of Castle Teravinea close to everyone I loved. My quarters were ground level with access to a small private garden. There was no excuse for my self-pity. No one could be more fortunate than I. But the stress of our upcoming ceremony, and that I couldn't see Ansel, pulled at me.

Before I could dwell on my darkening mood any longer, my stomach reminded me I hadn't eaten since earlier that morning. I glanced at the bell pull across the room and shook my head. I didn't think I would ever get used to summoning any of the staff to serve me in my quarters. Besides, I needed to get out of my room for a bit, so I decided to go down to the kitchen and find myself something to eat.

I took the less-traveled hallways and servants' route. Sneaking in the back way, I scanned the kitchen. The fires roared, the cooks bustled as they prepared for the coming feast. I made every effort to stay out of their way, hoping maybe they were too busy to notice

D. Maria Trimble

me. I'd no sooner stepped into the room when, like ripples in a pond, one dropped to a curtsy, another followed with a bow and soon they crowded around me, bobbing and asking how they can serve me. I struggled for patience as I tried to make them understand I preferred to find my own fare.

"As you were. Please, go back to your duties." I tried to sound authoritative, but felt miserably ineffective. They curtsied a few more times before returning to their chores.

Clenching my teeth, I maneuvered around them and headed toward the back corner of the kitchen. I reached a table that attracted my attention. It was loaded with breads and cheeses. As I reached to take a small loaf, I looked up and caught my breath.

"Ansel! What are you doing here?" My heart leaped as he entered from the opposite direction, heading for the same table.

My betrothed looked nearly as surprised as I.

"I suppose the same thing you're doing." He closed the gap between us and pulled me close.

Low gasps came from some of the women in the kitchen.

"Ansel, we're not supposed to see each other."

"It's not like we planned meeting here. But it would be a waste not to take advantage."

He flashed a devious smile and brought his lips to mine. Exclamations echoed louder from the kitchen workers. I ignored them and took equal advantage of the situation.

"You know this is bad luck." Fiona's voice interrupted my perfect moment.

Ansel and I broke apart, my eyes wide with guilty discovery. Fiona stood with her hands on her hips.

Before I could defend myself she started in, "Amáne, we discussed this today. I specifically reminded you that you two cannot see each other until —"

Black Castle

Her face went red as she turned toward Ansel. She executed a deep curtsy. "My Lord, I beg your pardon. I didn't mean to ... that is, I'm not telling you what to do in your castle. It's just that ... well ... you understand ... tradition and all."

Ansel cut in. "Fiona, it was a chance meeting." He scowled. "Tradition be hanged. I haven't seen Amáne for days." He gave me another quick kiss in defiance. "Who thought up that ridiculous convention, anyway?"

Fiona and I exchanged a glance. He'd repeated what I said to her earlier, nearly word-for-word.

A bit flustered, she conceded, "It does seem quite silly when it's one's own ceremony. I remember feeling the same way three days before Kail and I said our vows." She tipped her head at us. "Chance meeting or not, it seems to me you didn't waste the opportunity."

Fiona smiled then, and said almost to herself, "But I really can't fault you two."

She curtsied again as she grabbed my arm. "If you'll excuse us King Ansel, I'll take your lady and hope that there are no more breaks in our customs. It's bad luck."

I grabbed a lump of cheese and turned a pained look at Ansel as Fiona dragged me away.

CHAPTER FOUR

Two days remained before the wedding. The endless fittings, questions and final decisions I had to make proved to be a torture for me. The only thing that kept me from breaking the accursed custom was the fact that at least Ansel and I could communicate through our dragons. Fiona had no power to prohibit that. Maybe I'll confess it to her in the future, but in the mean time, it gave me great pleasure to bend tradition.

Fiona had entreated me to not leave the castle. In fact, she barely approved of me leaving my chambers. And even more aggravating, I knew she had a host of the castle staff keeping an eye on me, ready to report to her should I happen to encounter my betrothed. Many of the workers were superstitious, so they didn't take lightly the supposed curse of bad luck for breaking the tradition. If misfortune should befall their employers, it would stand to reason it would affect them as well. It occurred to me Fiona had solicited their help, even before my meeting with Ansel, else how would she have arrived at just the right moment to catch us? I loved Fiona dearly, but when she made her mind up

Black Castle

against or for something, she could be quite stubborn. I giggled at that thought.

I suppose no one can outdo me in stubbornness.

Restlessly pacing my room, I stomped my foot in frustration, then paused. A satisfying smile grew on my face. Throwing open my wardrobe, I reached toward the back and brought out a disheveled pile of clothing. I snickered as I slipped on my most worn tights and tunic, threw on a stained brown cape and pulled the hood low over my face.

"Eshshah, the wedding is the day after tomorrow. I need to get away for a few hours. Meet me outside Forest Gate and we can go for a quick flight. With all the frenzy around here, they'll not look twice at a commoner in the hallways."

I dragged a side table to the bell pull so I could stand on it and reach high enough to cut a long length of the cord. Then I coiled it and stuck it in my satchel. A tray with some empty bowls from my breakfast lay on my desk. Grabbing the tray, I padded to my door, cracked it open and sneaked a peek up and down the corridor. Almost clear. A guard stood at the end of the hall to my right, but his back faced me. I slipped out, carrying my full tray and headed in the opposite direction, hoping I'd pass as a serving boy.

In no time I found myself outside the gate, pleased with the success of my escape. Stashing the tray and bowls behind a bush, I clambered onto Eshshah's back.

I took the bell pull cord in my right hand and swung it under Eshshah's neck, trying to catch it on its upward swing on the other side. After a few tries, I finally managed to grab it. The length was just long enough for me to secure it around her neck. I couldn't chance going to the saddlery room for all of her equipment. Riding bareback was a rare thrill I shared with her, but I wasn't foolish enough to fly without something on which to hold.

In my haste to leave my chambers, I'd forgotten my breastplate and helmet. If the Healer, or Ansel knew I flew without, I would hear of it for days. I don't want to imagine the scowls on their faces if they knew I also flew with just a cord around Eshshah's neck. That vision evaporated the second Eshshah launched into the air. Exhilarated, I laughed out loud.

We soared over the river and headed toward the woods on the other side. The wind whipped at my hair. Eshshah and I glided low over the forest, riding the warm air currents. Then, with powerful strokes of her wings, she ascended higher. I closed my eyes and filled my lungs with the cool invigorating air.

"Eshshah, aren't we near where Charna hunts? Why don't you summon him?"

Charna Yash-churka was the mutant black lizard with whom I also shared a link.

Galtero, the deposed ruler of Teravinea, had attempted to breed dragons that would be loyal to him. The resulting species resembled lizards rather than dragons. Charna was one of those lizards. His tattoo-like mark on my ankle proved Galtero achieved some of the dragon traits he tried to emulate. I held the position as the only dragon rider in history to be twice-linked.

It had repulsed me each time I looked at the linking mark. That is, until my second encounter with the black lizard in Galtero's arena of death. Charna had saved my life from the other monster lizard pitted against me.

Filthy and ugly when I first encountered the mistreated beast, Charna now proved to be quite an imposing creature. Although he'll never be a sleek dragon, with his thick neck, stocky legs and wings that would never carry him, he and I still had a connection.

The black lizard's new life of freedom in the nearby forest

had refined him noticeably. His ebony scales gleamed, and because of the rich game in the forest, he no longer had the putrid odor of his earlier days.

Eshshah and I glided over the tree tops to a clearing and spiraled down to where Charna waited for us. I marveled at his size. He'd nearly tripled since our first meeting.

I still couldn't understand his primitive tongue, but Eshshah translated for me.

Enjoying the sun, he rolled onto his back and wriggled in the dirt. His actions reminded me of horses I'd seen rolling in pleasure. I laughed at his antics. When he rose, I noticed a few of his dark scales were left on the ground.

Picking one up, I examined it. Longer than it was wide, it fit the length of my hand. Similar to other dragon scales, the side that attached to his body ended in two spikes, the other end had a rounded point.

"Eshshah, do you think Charna's scales exhibit the properties of his name, like other dragon scales?"

"He does seem to show a lot of similar dragon traits. I would think that if mine could start a fire, Sovann's turn into gold and Sitara's scales illuminate, his should behave likewise. But, with a name meaning black lizard, I couldn't think what his scales would manifest."

"Let's find out." I held the scale close to my face and took a breath to whisper Charna's name.

"Amáne, wait. Don't you think another dragon rider should run this experiment with you? We don't know what to expect."

I laughed. "Eshshah, thank you for your concern, but you're too cautious. I'll ask another rider, or even the Healer once we get back. I just want to do a little test on my own. Nothing bad will happen."

She gave me a flat look. "Then don't put any power into your whisper. Say his name gently."

"Of course. Good idea, my beautiful dragon."

With the ebony scale in my palm, I brought it back up to chin level, and contemplating gentle thoughts, I said, "Charna Yashchurka."

A thin column of grey smoke oozed from the scale. The column divided into wispy tendrils that darkened as they rose. The smell of sulfur assaulted my nose. I pulled my face back and watched in fascination as the wisps entwined and, even though the air hadn't stirred, they curled toward me.

"Amáne," Eshshah's thoughts echoed her trepidation, "throw it down. Back away."

Her voice came as if from a long distance. I stood mesmerized. A terror filled my heart. I couldn't move. My hand jerked. The scale dropped. That didn't stop the probing tendrils. Like skeletal hands, they stretched out toward me and circled my head. They entered my nose and mouth.

A scream lodged in my throat as my sight went dark. Even in the blackness I could see shapes begin to form. Visions of my worst nightmares circled and moved in toward me. Fear tightened its grip on my chest. Panic roared inside. I couldn't pull myself from the blackness. A terrifying wail rang in my ears. It came from me.

I crouched and drew my dagger. Slashing out, the blade passed through the wraiths without effect. I turned and ran, swinging the dagger wildly in the air.

Talons closed around my waist and lifted me from the ground. I kicked and thrust my blade at my attacker. A warm wind blew in my face and I inhaled a familiar spicy aroma. Calmness enveloped me. The specters dissipated. My eyes opened to Eshshah's face inches from mine. She hummed her calming tune as she breathed again on me.

I wiped my eyes with the back of my hand. "Eshshah, what just happened?" Tremors swept through my body. It felt like my blood had been drained.

My dragon put me down gently. When she let go, I grasped her talons for balance.

"Charna's scales are quite powerful," she said. "It was as if you were caught in the Shadows."

Eshshah's distress filled me with guilt. "That was not the Shadows, Eshshah. I've been there. They don't hold the terror I just felt. It was more like a nightmare, but one in which I was fully awake."

I raised my arms up to her. She brought her head down to mine. "Once again," I said, "you proved to be the smarter of the two of us. And once again, I should have listened to you. When are you going to give up on me?"

She shook her head slowly.

My eyes swept to Charna. He shifted from one foot to the other, his head swung back and forth. I headed toward him, but still hadn't gained full control of my legs. He closed the distance between us. His dark eyes reflected anguish.

I exuded calmness to ease his distress. Pressing my forehead on his nose, I said, "Charna, no, this was not your fault. I'll be fine. Please don't act so wretched." Eshshah translated as I spoke. "Listen, we just found your scales exhibit a profound trait. A very valuable property. It may save one of our lives once we learn more about it. I'm going to bring some of your scales to the Healer. She'll know how to test them and how to harness the trait for our good. This is wonderful news, Charna."

I patted his large head and turned to Eshshah for affirmation. "You're too pale, Amáne. Let's get you back to the castle."

Eshshah breathed her healing breath on me once more. We returned to the spot where more of Charna's scales lay. I picked up all I could find, put them in my satchel and prepared to mount. My strength not yet restored, Eshshah had to stoop low and Charna gave me a boost with his head. Once up, I slipped both hands under the cord around Eshshah's neck and held tight before giving her the okay.

"Thank you Eshshah," I said to her once she dropped me off at Forest Gate. "I'm glad we did this."

"I'm just thankful nothing worse happened to you. Will you be all right? I can summon a rider to escort you back to your room."

"What? And listen to a lecture the whole way back?" I shook my head. "I'll be fine. I'm just a little light-headed. Eshshah, please, don't give me that guilty look. This adventure is entirely my responsibility."

"Your color hasn't returned, either."

"I'm fine, Eshshah. Forgive me for the bother I am to you." I smiled. She breathed on me once more before nudging me gently through the gate.

I pulled the hood of my cape down over my face, retrieved the tray I'd hidden and made my way through the hallways back to my chambers.

As I crossed a corridor, I caught a glimpse of Ansel and Fiona talking at the other end. Ansel faced in my direction and looked up just as I halted in the middle of the wide hallway. A slight smile turned his lips.

How does he know it's me?

Thanks to the shadow of my hood, he couldn't see my face clearly, which I was certain, still remained pale. It would surely have drawn his concern. Fiona must have caught his distraction because she started to turn her head when I ducked around the corner. The last thing I needed was to bear Fiona's admonitions.

Back in my room, I threw off my cape and gaped at myself in the looking glass. A frightful image stared back. Not only was my skin pallid, my eyes had dark circles under them. No wonder Eshshah seemed so concerned. I exhaled at the thought of Ansel's reaction if I hadn't been shadowed by my cape.

Then a frightening thought struck me. "Eshshah, what if I still look like this for my wedding?"

"We'll make sure you don't. A bath and a rest should do you well."

Eshshah was right. A hot soak set all to right. My nightmare receded behind me. My eyes were left with only a trace of their haunted appearance.

I summoned the Healer. She was the only family I had since I'd lost my mother. Not actually blood family, but my guardian and so much more. She and her husband, Gallen, both dragon riders, trained Eshshah and me when we first became linked as dragon and rider. Thinking back, it seemed like someone else's life so long ago.

I let the Healer into my room and gave her a warm hug. When she pulled back, she studied my face.

Tipping her head, she said, "Amáne, are you ill? Is that why you called for me?"

I should have known nothing gets past her.

I shook my head. "No, Healer, I'm fine, but come sit here and I'll tell you of our discovery."

Her brows lifted. She eyed me suspiciously.

I told her of what I had gone through, and passed on my findings about Charna Yash-churka's ebony scales.

She remained silent and seemed quite riveted by my narrative. After answering all of her questions, I endured the Healer's reprimand for my foolishness. I deserved it.

I'd placed Charna's scales in a small pouch which I handed to her. She hung it on her belt and stood to leave.

Taking my face in her hands, she peered into my eyes. The Healer had a way of searching deep as if she looked into my very core. Satisfied, she wrapped me in her strong arms. "You'll be fine."

A smile in her voice, she said, "Although I question your decision to delve into this in such haste, I believe this is a significant discovery. I'll keep you apprised of our findings."

I shut the door after her and stumbled to my bed. Exhaling in relief, I knew she would move forward to discover the benefits of Charna's scales.

CHAPTER FIVE

As a slew of attendants fussed about me in the early morning hours of my wedding day, the Healer entered my chambers and stood at the doorway. Her eyes glistened.

"Amáne, your mother would be so proud. You look beautiful." Her words came in a choking whisper.

"You're quite striking yourself, Healer." I put my hand out to her. My attendants parted so she could get to me. She kissed my forehead and then both cheeks, as was our custom.

I sighed. "Healer, I'm so nervous. So many people with their attention focused on me. What if I trip or do something embarrassing?"

The Healer laughed. "I'll be right next to you to make sure I deliver you safely to Ansel. You can cling to him after that. Stop your worrying. Do what you do best. Close your eyes and pretend no one is there."

I smiled. She knew me so well.

"And if that's not terror enough," I continued, "Fiona has cinched me so tightly, I'm afraid I won't be able to breathe. She and Lali have spent the last two hours fussing over this mass of silk and jewels and ribbons. It seems so irresponsible of me to wear such extravagance."

"You will have to get used to it, I'm afraid." She laughed. "Need I remind you, this is a royal wedding. Your people expect nothing less."

"My people. Oh Healer, it's all too much for me." My voice cracked, my eyes filled.

At that moment, Eulalia burst in the door — my lady-in-waiting. I called her by her informal name, Lali. She had been assigned by Ansel to attend me on my first visit to his manor. As Ansel put it, she was the only one of his staff that could 'handle me.' That still remained true.

"Lady Amáne, it's nearly time. Oh no, please, no crying. Haven't we been through this already?" She picked up a linen from the dressing table, and holding my chin, dabbed the corners of my eyes. "Do you not remember how we went over this way back when? Crying will mar your beautiful face. Do you want your people to see you with red eyes, or worse yet, a red nose?"

My people. I closed my eyes and exhaled.

Eulalia kept up her banter. "What will they wonder? That their future queen regrets her position? Or that she got in a spat with their king? Is she ill? Lady Amáne, at the risk of telling you what to do, you must smile and nod your head and have all believe that you were born to your position in society, and that you love the attentions. I know how you feel about it, I did not meet you yesterday. But you must not allow your fears to show. Relax, or at least give the pretense of a noble at ease. That is what is expected of you."

How can she speak so incessantly? But I love her dearly.

Lali stepped back and studied me. "Fiona surely did a magnificent job with your dress, m'lady. She's used the finest

Black Castle

Serislan silk, I'll wager, and dyed it a perfect silver. You'll excuse me for saying, because I know you'll object, but I'll say it anyway. It does wonders for your femininity — or should I say it improves your lack of. That bodice actually gives you a noticeable bust line. Not the boy-like shape you seem to prefer." She eyed the stomacher, an inverted triangle of lace, goldwork and jewels that started at my bust and pointed down to just past my hips.

I rolled my eyes, which didn't stop Lali. "And the latest fashion in sleeves." She primped the ruffles at my shoulders, and ran her hand down my arm where the fabric hugged down to a point at the back of my hand and looped around my thumb. A chain of gemstones belted around my waist and hung down to about my knees.

Lali stopped and cleared her throat. "Ah, but I ramble on." She gave a nervous laugh as she turned to the Healer, who stood with eyebrows raised and mouth open, looking like she had tried to get in a word.

Eulalia curtsied, "Lady Healer, my apologies. I'll hold my tongue. I have the royal jewels here to put on Lady Amáne and then she is all yours."

"Thank you, Lali. The carriage is waiting to take us to the field where Eshshah awaits."

Lali fastened Ansel's mother, Queen Fiala's, priceless necklace of pearls and emeralds around my neck, and hung the matching earrings. Completing the set was the circlet she placed on my head, on which a smaller emerald pendant adorned my forehead. She paced around me in admiration, making sure not a thread or hair was out of place.

A tap on the door brought my head around. A maid opened it to Fiona's younger sisters, the twins, Rio and Mila.

How did I miss that they had become such beautiful young ladies?

They stepped in the room and their eyes widened, their jaws dropped.

"Amáne," they whispered simultaneously. "... Lady Amáne," they corrected.

I laughed. "I will always be just Amáne to you."

I opened my arms to invite them for a hug. They stepped forward. Behind them, to my delight, a girl about their same age drew near — Kira, a young friend whom I'd met on a slave ship. But that was another nightmare I preferred to forget. Kira held a special place in my heart. A fortnight ago Ansel and I had flown to Kep, in the northern part of Serislan, to pick her up, along with her mother. The twins had instantly bonded with Kira.

The three girls approached slowly and placed soft kisses on my face.

"Fiona sent us to help you to the carriage," Rio said.

"We'll carry your train," Mila added.

"She said to tell you she'll meet you where Eshshah waits," Kira finished.

Chapter Six

I stepped out of the carriage and gasped in delight.

"Eshshah! You're gorgeous. Look at you."

The horns on her head had been wrapped in gold, as had the barb at the end of her tail. Colorful silk ribbons were woven down her long graceful neck, her talons painted in a pearlescent lacquer.

She wore a specially-made saddle, upholstered in silk. I had argued against a side-saddle. Gown or no gown, I would sit my saddle as a proper dragon rider. It was a small victory for me, when Fiona acceded to my wishes. The saddle was small and light, like the fighting saddle. It secured me at the foot pegs, instead of the thigh straps of the larger saddle.

I ran to Eshshah as fast as my silken attire would allow. The three girls rushed to help keep my gown from trailing on the ground. I held my arms in invitation to my dragon. Eshshah brought her large head down to mine for me to place a kiss against her nose.

"Eshshah, you are the most beautiful of all."

She rumbled her pleasure and hummed a calming tune for me.

"My lady," said Fiona with a mischievous air. She curtsied. "Are you pleased with her adornments?"

"Of course! She's beautiful."

I swatted at my friend. "Fiona, if you ever call me my lady again, or curtsy, I promise I'll send you back to Dorsal!"

We locked in a hug, both of us as giddy as school girls.

Mila, Kira and Rio got to work folding my train, preparing me to ride. I maneuvered to Eshshah's foreleg. She crouched as low as she could, allowing me to pull myself into the saddle. I struggled with my gown until I settled in the seat. The girls stood on Eshshah's forelegs and arranged my dress, then buckled my feet in the foot pegs.

Satisfied, Fiona, the girls and the Healer stepped back and gazed up at me. They placed their forefinger and thumb together to form an "O." With the other three fingers straight, they placed their hand on their heart and gave me a crisp dragon salute. I nodded at my friends. To the Healer, I returned the dragon salute.

Both Eshshah and I looked up at the same time.

I took in a breath and said, "Ansel and Sovann have taken flight. See how the light plays off Sovann's golden scales. He gleams like the sun."

The girls squealed in delight.

I could hear cheers and shouts from the wedding venue on the other side of the castle as Ansel and his golden dragon spiraled higher.

"We have to leave now," said the Healer. "We'll see you over there." She beamed with pride at Eshshah and me before she turned and rushed toward the waiting carriage.

"Well, Eshshah," I said, "it's just you and me. This is the point where I usually fall apart."

Black Castle

"You can't, Amáne. Not today. Besides that's only for quests and battles." I smiled at her humor.

I watched as Ansel and Sovann descended. The cheers became louder as they disappeared from my line of sight. My pulse accelerated. I took in a deep breath and exhaled slowly.

"I'm getting married, Eshshah! I'm getting married! I never thought I'd see this day. I never thought I'd say this is the best day of my life. I'm so nervous."

Eshshah's amusement reverberated in her chest once again. Then she announced, "Amáne, it's time."

She spread her wings, and with a powerful thrust of her hind legs, we took to the air. I closed my eyes and forgot my fears. For however long my life proves to be, I will always delight in the gloriousness of flying with my dragon.

As we circled higher, I caught my first glimpse of the mass of people gathered for this special day.

"Eshshah," I said out loud. There were still times I preferred to use my voice.

"I'm with you, Amáne." Her comforting warmth filled me.

High above the crowds, I surveyed the festival colors of the City of Teravinea. Although I knew it to be a beautiful city, its transformation for our celebration of vows left me in awe. For as far as I could see, the city resonated with vitality, as if our wedding had brought it back to its former glory. Even the vineyards seemed to glow with renewed life.

Eshshah flew slowly as we circled above the crowd. Countless faces below us turned up to watch our approach.

If Ansel and Sovann were up here with us, I would beg for us to keep flying. But that was a wish to no avail. We spiraled down. The guests delighted in the sight of Eshshah's graceful descent.

I caught a glimpse of Ansel just arriving at the arch. My heart beat wildly. I couldn't take my eyes off of him. Gallen took his place to Ansel's right.

The wooden archway, which stood behind King Tynan of Serislan, who performed the ceremony, was fitted with a door. This door would remain closed until we pledged our troth. After our pledge, King Tynan would open it and invite Ansel and me to walk through. This signified we'd begun our new lives together.

Eshshah touched down lightly. Fiona, along with Kira, Mila and Rio rushed over to assist me. They released my feet from the foot pegs. Thinking it was the most fluid way to descend, I swung my leg in front of me to dismount.

The train of my gown had become partially unbound in flight. As I tried to gracefully slide down to Eshshah's foreleg, a fold of the train caught on the foot peg on the opposite side. Instead of alighting graciously, I found myself dangling from my saddle, in the most awkward pose.

Ohs and ahs and other echoes of astonishment came from the guests on my side of Eshshah. Heat rose in my face. Thankfully, Eshshah stood between Ansel and the spectacle I made of myself as I hung suspended a half a length above the ground.

I think it was Kira, who in a panic, ran to the other side of Eshshah. Without warning, she released the fabric that held me. I tumbled in a heap behind Eshshah's foreleg. It had been a while since I'd seen the Healer move so quickly. She rushed to my side and pulled me to my feet.

I was mortified. But when I noticed Rio's, Mila's and Kira's faces, all of them had the same wide-eyed, open-mouthed look of shock. I couldn't help but start giggling at their absurd expressions.

Fiona eyed me warily.

Black Castle

"Maybe you really aren't cut out for this sort of life, Amáne," she said. "Have you gone mad?"

I laughed harder. After staring at me for a moment, she broke into laughter. At which point the twins and Kira joined in.

"All right, ladies," the Healer said. "We have several kingdoms of guests waiting to see you walk up that aisle. Any more time here and Ansel will think you've changed your mind."

Everyone sprang into action. Kira, Rio and Mila puffed and primped and rearranged my gown until Fiona nodded her satisfaction.

We stepped away from Eshshah, who took to wing as soon as we cleared. I sent her my love as I watched her rise. She would fly to join Sovann in a place of honor behind King Tynan, on the other side of the arched door. It relieved me to know she would be so close. I could look upon her should my panic rise. Eshshah was a balm for my nerves.

Standing with Eshshah and Sovann would be Charna Yashchurka. His ebony scales a sharp contrast beside Sovann's golden glow and Eshshah's iridescent fiery scales. I beamed with pride at the thought of these three magnificent dragons.

The other dragons perched atop the city walls, embellishing our already-impressive surroundings. I felt their curiosity in the strange customs of humans. Fiona had told me they would play a part in the ceremony, but kept the details from me.

We moved the short distance to the wedding aisle, paved in white cobblestones.

Most of the guests hadn't seen my embarrassing dismount, but I'm sure an account would soon spread from those that did. I lifted my chin in my best interpretation of a dignified air.

Of course the entire kingdom could not attend the ceremony, but the guest list was necessarily extensive. I could thank Fiona and her assistants a thousand times and it would not suffice. Deciding the attendees was a matter of protocol, etiquette and of course, political decorum. I gave very little input, but paid great attention in an effort to learn diplomatic formalities. The fact that many esteemed guests had the honor of arriving via dragonback proved to be a good move in regards to foreign relations.

I scanned the crowd. So many rich colors — purples and blues. The extravagant clothing of the privileged amazed me, as if in competition. The ladies in particular, displayed their finest emeralds, sapphires and diamonds, each trying to outdo the other and make known their status.

"Eshshah," I said in thought transference, "I don't know if I'll ever understand the aristocracy. I'm not sure I want to."

"Amáne, I believe you are now considered part of it."

I smiled at her revelation and brought my thoughts back to the moment. Ahead of me, stood twenty dragon riders who had marched up the paved aisle in two rows. A pair faced each other at even intervals. Mila, Rio and Kira held my train. The Healer positioned herself to my right. She clasped a jeweled chain around my wrist from which hung a silver silken cord. Placing her left hand over my right, she draped the cord loosely over our joined hands.

Fiona signaled the musicians, who took up their lutes, dulcimers and flutes, and struck up our traditional march. My heart pounded against my chest. I froze. My feet refused to move. The Healer gently tugged my hand as Eshshah prompted me to start. The aisle seemed hopelessly long.

What are the chances I could make it all the way without another mishap?

It was then my eyes met Ansel's as he waited at the arch. Nothing else mattered. There was only Ansel. My fear no longer ruled.

Black Castle

He stood resplendent in his wedding attire — a white shirt with billowing sleeves, intricate embroidery weaving its way down each arm; dragonscale breastplate, constructed from Sovann's golden scales, buckled over a royal blue velvet silk tunic; white tights and dragonscale boots; his father's jeweled sword at his side and a golden circlet on his head.

I forgot to breathe.

"Slow down, child," the Healer whispered out of the corner of her mouth.

"Sorry."

As we passed each set of dragon riders, they gave us the dragon salute. I kept my eyes locked on Ansel, which was probably the only reason I remained upright.

The Healer delivered me without further misadventure. She unwrapped the silken cord and left it to hang from my wrist, then stepped back as Ansel offered me his arm. His radiant smile, nearly made my knees buckle. I hooked my right arm around his left arm and clung to him, tightly.

As calm as Ansel seemed on the outside, I could feel his nervousness. I don't know why, but for some reason it relieved my own tension. I brought my other hand over his wrist and smiled up at him to help put him to ease.

Then I remembered the proper position Fiona had drilled into me. Promptly, I released my grip and placed my right forearm over his left forearm, my hand gently over his. Exhaling slowly, I allowed a bit of my healing powers to help us both. Our eyes met and we shared a silent giggle. Hopefully, Fiona wouldn't have caught my error.

Ansel and I advanced the remaining three paces to stand before King Tynan of Serislan. I concentrated on breathing.

King Tynan stood regally upon a dais, three steps above us. A look of pride lit his face. He was impressive in his red velvet robes edged with a rare spotted white fur. An ornate golden crown circled his white hair.

He began in a resounding voice, "Esteemed guests, I stand before you, as close ally to the Kingdom of Teravinea. I proudly take part in this ceremony of vows to join King Ansel Drekinn to Amáne of Duer and Catriona.

"I have a history with Teravinea. King Emeric, this young man's father, was my friend. His tragic death, my loss as well. He and his wife, the beautiful Queen Fiala, would be so proud of their son, I can assure you of that."

King Tynan paused and scanned the masses before resuming. "And this beautiful young lady, who will be your queen, has played an exceptional role in the successful alliance of our kingdoms."

My eyes went wide. My hand tightened on Ansel's.

Is he going to start telling those stories now?

"Twice now, she has saved the lives of my heirs, and I am forever indebted to this kingdom because of her bravery and sense of duty."

He cleared his throat and huffed a small laugh.

"Ah, but those are tales for another time, let us proceed with the ceremony."

I heaved a sigh of relief and loosened my hold on Ansel's hand.

"Lords and Ladies, citizens of Teravinea and guests from other realms," Tynan continued. "We gather here at the request of King Ansel and Lady Amáne. They desire that you witness the pledging of their troth. Before you, they take their vows. From you, they ask your blessing."

The king nodded at us.

BLACK CASTLE

Ansel faced me, moved closer and took both of my hands in his. The silver cord hung between us. He brought my hands to his lips and pressed a gentle kiss. I blushed. A warmth spread through me. My body trembled. When our eyes met, I lost myself in the depth of his. I wanted to slow down time, to memorize every second, every word, and yet before I knew it, our vows were spoken.

King Tynan's booming voice startled me as he said, "Before the exchange of the rings, the couple wishes to display their total commitment to each other in a symbol of dedication. They bring back an age-old Teravinean tradition that had been banned for the last twenty years, the Washing of the Feet."

Murmurs went through the crowd. I noted sounds of excitement and approval. The king's eyes swept over the guests.

"For those of you not of Teravinea, I will explain. The Washing of the Feet had always been a ritual in Teravinean weddings. It is based on the idea of service to each other. Affirmation that King Ansel will honor and respect Lady Amáne, and she, likewise, will honor and respect King Ansel." Tynan nodded at Ansel and then at me, before he continued. "The act demonstrates a humility of heart and character, kneeling before your spouse. In turn, it communicates, 'I will accept your help.' That is, indeed, a test of love when you realize you need each other's support."

A woman with a beautiful voice began to sing a traditional ballad as an attendant brought forward a chair. Another carried a fine porcelain basin and a pitcher made especially for the ceremonial Washing of the Feet. A scene of dragons flying above Castle Teravinea decorated the set in gold leaf.

These items meant even more to me as they were crafted by my mother, Catriona. She had been a potter in this city, and had made much of the ceramic ware for the House of Drekinn when they ruled. This set was found in a storage room in the castle, untouched for decades. It comforted my heart to know a work of art from my mother's hands would be here with me on this extraordinary day. She had been the most important person in my life.

I also had an item of my father's, whom I never had the chance to get to know well. I could feel Duer's presence as I carried a small dagger of his sheathed in the folds of my gown. Without much protest, Fiona had fashioned a special pocket for it. She knew how much it meant to me.

I lowered myself onto the chair. Rio, Mila and Kira approached to help with my gown. Ansel knelt before me and removed my slippers.

Holding my feet over the basin, he poured the water from the pitcher and tenderly washed them. The guests in the front row were close enough to see my right foot where my linking mark from Charna entwined around my ankle. Like Eshshah's image on my arm, his was a stylized image of himself — a tattoo of sorts. I heard soft whispering and some astonished inhales.

Ansel gazed up at me, "My heart, my love, my Amáne, I kneel before you to make a pledge for all to witness. I promise to always defend you, to honor our union, and love you more each day than I did the day before. I will trust you and respect you; laugh and dance with you when you are joyful; share your tears with you when you are sorrowful. You will always be the color in my day, the salt of my sustenance, until the day I meet my ancestors."

I smiled at him as I wiped a tear from my cheek.

Rio handed him a towel. As Ansel dried my feet, he caressed my ankle. I inhaled sharply as the warmth of his touch rose from my foot to my face. His lips turned up as he replaced my slippers, knowing the effect he had on me. I shot him an embarrassed glance with a hint of a warning, but I couldn't keep the smile from my face.

Ansel stood and offered his hand. We traded positions and I knelt at his feet. Thankfully, I didn't have much trouble removing his boots.

As the water flowed over his feet, I drew my eyes to his and recited, "Ansel, my love and my life, I kneel before you to make a pledge for all to witness. I promise to love you unconditionally, to respect you, to care for and protect you, to comfort and encourage you. In you I have found a great treasure, a faithful friend, my sturdy shelter. Your friendship and love is beyond price. Where you go I will go, where you stay I will stay. You are my heart and my love until the day I meet my ancestors."

I took the towel Mila offered and began to dry Ansel's feet. Knowing the front rows had a good view, I arranged the towel to conceal my action. I ran my hand softly from his heel up his calf. Biting my lower lip, I offered him a teasing look.

I'd witnessed Ansel enough times in affairs of state and official ceremonies, and his composure always impressed me. I wasn't sure of the reaction I expected, but the passion in his smoldering eyes took me by surprise. His self control momentarily interrupted, he huffed out a short breath. I swallowed and tried to appear smug, but it didn't stop the heat rising in my face. Dropping my eyes, I assisted him with his boots.

Ansel placed his hands beneath my elbows, and helped me to my feet. Considering the dress into which I'd been sewn, I couldn't have risen without him. With his eyes upon me, the urge to tip my face up to his overcame me. His burning expression made it difficult to maintain the refined behavior expected of me.

Eshshah's humor entered my thoughts. "Amáne, I'm surprised at your restraint."

Without a second thought, I pulled Ansel's face to mine and kissed him soundly on the lips. Ignoring the gasps from the guests, and some cat calls from the back of the crowd, I pulled away, raised my chin and placed my arm in the proper position over Ansel's. I didn't dare gaze in his direction as I regained my composure. I managed a dignified expression, as if my brash action had never occurred.

"Eshshah, you shouldn't have encouraged me," I said to her in thought transference.

She rumbled her laughter.

"That's my girl," Ansel whispered out of the side of his mouth.

I responded with a small shrug.

We turned back to King Tynan, who, with eyebrows raised, shook with silent laughter.

He paused a moment longer and took in a few breaths as he attempted to collect himself. Then he continued in an even voice. "King Ansel and Lady Amáne, do you have the rings?"

Gallen stepped forward and handed them to Tynan, who held them up above his head. Another song began, the blessing of the rings song. As the singer's voice faded, King Tynan handed Ansel my ring.

Ansel recited as he slipped the ring on my finger, "Because this ring is perfectly symmetrical, it signifies the perfection of true love. As I place it on your finger, I give you all that I am and ever hope to be."

Tynan handed Ansel's ring to me. I faced Ansel and said, "Because this ring has no end or beginning, it signifies the continuation of true love. As I place it on your finger, I give you all that I am and ever hope to be."

The king descended the steps of the dais and motioned for me to place my right arm over Ansel's left arm, in the same position in which we had started. He took the silken cord and wrapped it three times around our hands, then turned us to face the guests as he announced, "Lords and ladies, may I be the first to introduce to you, King Ansel and his wife, Queen Amáne of Drekinn. You may now seal your vows with a kiss." Under his breath he said, "Again."

Ansel and I turned to each other. With his free hand at the small of my back, he pressed me close. Our lips met. We left no doubt that our vows were sealed.

King Tynan waited patiently, then continued, "Please walk through the arched door to begin your new life."

He stepped aside as Ansel and I climbed the three steps toward the door. Ansel opened it and we passed through. Eshshah and Sovann waited on the lawns that spread out on the other side of the door. They lifted their heads to the sky and trumpeted with joy. Flames burst from their mouths and shot high into the air.

Cheers resounded through the crowd.

At that moment, the twenty-two dragons who had been perched on the city walls took flight, bellowing their responses to our dragons. They came together in a V formation and glided over the event. The sight, as well as the sound, was breathtaking.

We approached our dragons. After we unwrapped the silken cord from our hands, Ansel helped me gather my train and hook it over my arm as Fiona instructed. He gave me a boost up on Eshshah and secured my feet before he got astride Sovann. Eshshah and Sovann launched into the air to join the other dragons in an aerial dance, much to the delight of the guests. The musicians struck up a melody written expressly to accompany our flight.

"A large male dragon flew in before the ceremony," Eshshah informed me. "Sovann and I didn't recognize him."

"Why would a lone dragon come here?" I said. "All the riders now have a mount. There's no one with whom he can bond. Is he flying with us now?"

"No. We informed Braonán, who sent Calder and his dragon to investigate. They returned saying they couldn't find him."

"It's possible he just came to bring a gift from the Valley of Dragons and has headed back home. Everyone has been so busy, they probably overlooked telling us. We'll find out tomorrow when we open the gifts. I'm sure it's not anything we need to worry about."

After a few passes, Eshshah and Sovann veered off and headed for another part of the castle grounds. The other dragons continued their aerial show. We landed by a private entrance that led to where the feast was to be held.

Dismounting, I made my way to Eshshah's head. I held her fangs and leaned my forehead against her nose. She hummed her delight.

In thought transference, she said to Ansel and me, "Congratulations to you two. I wish you a long life. Never forget your troth today."

I kissed her and said, "There's no chance I will ever forget this day. Ever."

Ansel and I watched with pride as Eshshah and Sovann leaped into the air. My love for my dragon nearly overwhelmed me.

Feeling Ansel's eyes upon me, I turned and said, "What?"

"Have I ever told you that I love you?"

"Hmm, I think it's been quite a while. Probably nearly half an hour."

"I should do something about that."

Placing his hands on my waist, he pulled me close. I dropped my train and locked my fingers behind his neck. The heat of his

BLACK CASTLE

kiss sent a tremor through my body. It was as if a fire had ignited inside me.

"I like that you showed me, instead of telling me," I whispered.

"Then let me show you again," Ansel breathed. And he did, even more fervently.

"Oh, excuse us. We're sorry ... er. We'll just wait over there by the banquet hall door." Young voices broke into our embrace.

We parted to see Rio, Mila and Kira moving quickly back through the corridor.

Ansel and I laughed as we rushed to catch up.

"Girls," I called, "it's all right. Wait for us. We're ready."

We moved through the short corridor to meet the three girls at a set of large double doors. They fussed about my gown and spread the train as we waited for the signal to enter.

At last trumpets sounded, a herald announced, "All hail King Ansel and Queen Amáne!"

We stepped into the Great Hall. I gasped at the sight. Fabric banners of every color hung from the rafters. Tapestries that I'd never seen here at the castle decorated the walls. Colorful scenes of dragons and riders were woven in marvelous works of art.

"Do you like them?" asked Ansel. "They're gifts from King Tynan."

"They're magnificent. He must have an army of tapestry makers. If you agree, I'd love that one in our chambers."

I pointed to one that had attracted my attention. One depicting Sovann and Eshshah flying over Serislan castle.

"You can do anything you like, my queen."

The dragon riders again lined a path for us to follow to the other end of the hall. We stood on a thick, richly-woven rug about five paces long and four wide. A long line of guests queued to offer their felicitations. King Tynan, Gallen and the Healer stood with us in positions of honor. Neither Ansel nor I had parents who would normally have occupied that role.

The guests took their turns greeting us. I nodded, offered my hand, laughed lightly when appropriate and kept a polite smile until my face muscles hurt. The gentry, of course, had been first in line. Relief spread through me when I saw the dragon riders next in the queue, taking up the last of the well-wishers.

The first to approach was Braonán, who'd been the lead rider in charge of Ansel from the time Ansel was a small child. He saluted both of us with great pride.

Done with the stuffy aristocracy, I opened my arms to the large bear-of-a-man. He enclosed me and hugged me with more emotion than I'd ever seen from him. Calder followed suit and added a kiss to my forehead.

Next in line, was Avano. Another who had the responsibility of overseeing Ansel's upbringing. He was the last of the dragon riders to link before Eshshah and I came along.

Dragon riders lived very long lives. Avano looked only a bit older than Ansel, but he probably had seen at least fifty years. After Gallen, he was my favorite of all the riders.

With a flourish of his arm, Avano took a deep bow before me. "I offer my blessings and congratulations, my queen."

I stepped in and punched him in the chest.

With teeth clenched, I said, "If you ever bow to me again, Avano, I will use my queenly powers and command *off with your head*."

He threw his head back and burst into laughter. Wrapping his arms around me, he lifted me off my feet. My laugh came out as loud as his. Heads turned, but I didn't care.

BLACK CASTLE

The rest of the riders bid their good wishes in their turn and headed toward their table. My heart swelled with honor that the members of this extraordinary group were my friends, my brotherhood.

Fiona glided up and took Ansel's and my hands. "You did a beautiful job in the ceremony. Even you, Amáne, after you stopped clinging to King Ansel and took his hand like a proper bride."

"I was hoping you didn't catch that," I said.

"That wasn't the only thing I caught," Fiona said raising her eyebrows.

My eyes went wide.

"Delightfully scandalous," she whispered in my ear.

"I agree, Fiona," Ansel said.

It was her turn to stand in embarrassment.

"Ugh, I forgot about you riders and your hearing." Her musical laugh surrounded us.

"Speaking of scandalous, when can we be excused?" asked Ansel. "Please tell me we don't have to stay until the sun comes up."

"Patience, m'lord," she answered. "This is an early wedding. You'll be able to make your getaway around sunset. I'll tell you more about that when the time draws near."

Ansel squeezed my hand. I shot a nervous look at Fiona.

"Your guests are being ushered to their tables, please move to the high table and take your seats. Once you're seated, the feast will begin. Enjoy."

"Fiona, I want you to enjoy yourself, too. You're so busy, you're not celebrating with us."

"In truth, Amáne, I'm having the time of my life. Tomorrow I'll be bored and moping until you assign me another event."

"Then I'm afraid you'll have to mope for quite some time. The only thing I want to take part in after all this is ..." I shot a glance at Ansel, whose expression was expectant. "I mean ... that is ... oh ... er..."

Fiona tipped her head and smiled. "I can't help you with that, love."

I pressed my lips together and tugged Ansel to our seats at the high table. My eyes scanned the room and I realized the guests were standing by their places waiting for us to take our chairs. I sat quickly and Ansel followed.

The music changed cadence and the room bustled with servers. Delicious aromas wafted around us. Just then, I remembered I'd hardly eaten anything all day. My stomach called for attention. I sighed. This gown would not allow me to enjoy the amount of food I normally could consume. I decided to put my mind to something else.

"Ansel, I have a question."

"Yes, my beloved?"

"First I want to tell you I think your words to me were beautiful, but I'm not sure I understood what you meant when you said I was the salt of your sustenance. Are you sure you didn't mean the salt in your wounds?"

"Never," he laughed. "Since you seem to prefer being shown rather than told, let me show you."

He beckoned a serving maid to us. She curtsied and stood wide-eyed and nervous. Leaning toward her, he whispered something in her ear. Surprisingly, I couldn't hear what he told her. The young girl curtsied again as she backed away and hurried off.

My eyebrows came together and I lifted a shoulder. Ansel seemed amused.

The maid returned with a steaming plate of roasted meat that made my mouth water. At Ansel's gesture, she placed a slice on his plate. He cut a small piece and offered it to me. I closed my eyes and savored it with delight.

"Your chefs have outdone themselves," I said between chews, forgetting my manners.

"Our chefs, my love. You have to get used to it. All this is yours as well."

I laughed as I licked my lips.

He nodded to the girl and she served another slice from her platter. It looked just as enticing. I wondered at his apparent lesson, or possibly it was a Drekinn tradition that the groom feed the bride. I opened my mouth for the next burst of flavor.

As my teeth came together, my face scrunched up. The meat sat tasteless in my mouth. I couldn't, with any manners, spit it out, so I grabbed the goblet in front of me and tipped it back, forcing the insipid meat down my throat.

"What did they put in that meat?" I said choking.

Ansel couldn't hold his laughter. I had the feeling my reaction was just what he'd hoped for.

"That, my beloved, is the taste of meat with no salt or seasoning of any kind. Now do you know what I meant?"

I pinched his arm.

"Yes, now I understand, salt of my life," I laughed. "Lesson learned. This time I would rather you had simply told me."

CHAPTER SEVEN

Trays and bowls of meats, breads and cheeses continued to flow into the hall. Toward the end of the meal a clanking of knives on goblets rose from the dragon rider's table. I swung my eyes in their direction as they started chanting, "Tell us the tale. Tell us the tale."

By tradition, during a Teravinean vows celebration, the newly-joined couple is encouraged to tell the story of their first meeting and how it led to this day. I couldn't be sure the upper classes observed the same custom, but when you have a table full of riders insisting, the practice would carry on.

I noted most of the guests soon joined the riders in their chant. Those that weren't sure, took a quick glance at their neighbors and fell in with the rest.

Ansel stood and held up his goblet. I smiled as I recognized it was the ceramic goblet I had made for him for his eighteenth birthday. The one with the two dragons wrapped around the bowl, their tails entwined down the stem. He offered me his hand, which I took as I rose and stood close to him, raising my own goblet.

The attention of the entire hall drew to Ansel and me. My mouth went dry. Closing my eyes, I took a deep breath. If I kept my focus on my fellow dragon riders, I could actually manage an outward calm.

"Thank you, my esteemed guests," Ansel began in a resonant voice. "My bride and I are very pleased that you could join us in our celebration."

He turned to me, we toasted and drank, which was then repeated throughout the hall.

Ansel scanned the tables, a radiant smile on his face. An air of regal grace emanated from him. I gazed up at my husband with utmost pride.

"Lords and ladies, my fellow dragon riders have initiated a request for the tale."

The rider's table broke into shouts and clapping. If there is one thing my brotherhood of riders can do, it's adding an atmosphere of revelry to every occasion. I had no worries this would be a stuffy affair.

"As requested," Ansel continued, "we'll recount the circumstances of our meeting and what brought us to this most special day."

He turned to me. "If you'll allow me to start my lady?"

I nodded.

"The tale began for me the day I awoke to find myself shackled and chained in a cell in the dungeon of this very castle."

Most had never heard the story. Expressions of shock spread around the room. I marveled at the way Ansel could stir up emotion.

"I awaited my execution. It was my fortune Galtero happened to be away at the time of my capture, else I'd not be telling this tale. I paced the filthy chamber — my chains only allowed three steps in either direction — and cursed myself that my own foolishness had been the cause of my situation. Hope did not shine brightly in that cell. Not that I'd given up, but my outlook was bleak. The future of Teravinea did not bode well."

Ansel paused. I blinked back a tear.

He took a breath and went on. "A racket down the corridor put me on my guard. This meant either they'd come to take me to my end, or it could be my last chance of escape. I dropped down and took a position sitting on the floor, with my knees drawn up and my head resting on them. Someone unlatched my cell door and entered. He whispered my name. I stayed silent. Again, I heard my name, but didn't answer. This time it came from a closer distance.

"I watched out of the corner of my eye. It was a young boy who'd entered. He put his weapons down and approached slowly. Here was my chance. When he came close enough, I leaped up to strangle him with my chains. His speed surprised me. He evaded my attack, and turned to counter me."

I took my eyes from Ansel to survey the room. All the tables were silent. Even the serving people slowed their tasks, hanging on Ansel's words.

He continued, "Burning with anger that this slight boy could best me, I challenged him to unchain me and fight fairly. He, instead revealed my aunt, the Healer, had sent him to my rescue.

"To my shame, I broke foul on him. Cursing him, I accused him of lying and said my aunt wouldn't have sent a boy to do a man's job."

Ansel turned to me and nodded. I took up the story. "He was correct. His aunt didn't send a boy, she sent a girl ... me."

Heads tilted, eyebrows raised. A small rustle of whispers ran through the hall, like fallen leaves blowing across cobblestones.

"Don't fault your king for not recognizing a female."

I smiled at Ansel. The riders laughed.

BLACK CASTLE

"I was disguised as a male. Very convincingly, I'll add."

Words of affirmation came from my friends, stares of disbelief from my audience.

"It was my duty to get the Healer's nephew safely to where my dragon, Eshshah waited at the Castle Outpost. Between his stubbornness and mine, it's a wonder we actually survived. Only because of Eshshah were we able to navigate the corridors under the castle."

Ansel took over. "Of course she would leave out the fact that through my fault she was grievously wounded. We inadvertently found ourselves in a chamber occupied by a ferocious black lizard. The same you probably saw wandering the grounds at the ceremony."

Echoes of fear came from our guests. A woman stifled a scream.

I shook my head and shot a reprimanding glance at Ansel, "No need to fear the Black Lizard. He's as gentle as the other dragons. Charna was an experiment gone poorly. Created by Galtero in an effort to breed his own species of dragon, the poor lizard had been starved and mistreated. When live meat walked into his chambers, he sought to take advantage. I nearly lost my foot to him. Instead, his venomous bite, like a hatching dragon's bite, linked me to him."

I gestured for Ansel to continue.

"Even in her pain, Amáne kept up her ruse as a male. I couldn't help being impressed with her fortitude, or his fortitude," he shrugged, "as he tried to hide his pain and get me to safety. Unbeknownst to me, Eshshah directed us through the maze of passages several levels below. While admiring my rescuer's perseverance, I also questioned his sanity. He spoke with his dragon out loud instead of using thought transference. I was convinced he thought he heard voices."

"It seemed an impossible task, but we made it to the Castle Outpost," I said. "Since there had been no dragons in Teravinea in our lifetime, Eshshah and I decided we would introduce her to Ansel ... King Ansel ... slowly, so he wouldn't be alarmed. In retrospect, he deserved to be scared witless at that point."

Ansel and I turned to each other at the same time. A corner of his mouth lifted.

Laughter rippled through the hall.

"I was pleased to see his shock at coming face-to-face with a full-grown dragon, and at his look of incredulity when I removed my helmet and he realized I was a girl. But, then the surprise turned on me when my dragon bowed before my troublesome charge. Eshshah, being of the royal dragon line, recognized King Ansel as a Drekinn, true heir to the throne."

"I don't know whose eyes went wider, hers or mine," said Ansel. "Eshshah has remarkable healing powers, but could only give Amáne a quick treatment to subdue her pain. We had to leave before daylight. She endured a stressful three-hour flight back to the Dorsal Outpost where the Healer waited for us. It was during the day-and-a-half when my bride lay unconscious, that I discovered I was falling in love with this remarkable girl."

He pulled me close and kissed my forehead, then my lips. His kiss was like fire. The riders clapped and whistled. I blushed.

"To my vexation, she refused my advances and continued to reject me for quite some time."

My eyes scanned the hall and I couldn't mistake the disbelief reflecting on the women's faces, as if I couldn't be more of a dolt for refusing Ansel's attentions.

I jumped in, "I had a duty to protect King Ansel, and to train for an upcoming quest. We needed our kingdom back and I had to put my efforts into our mission, before I listened to my heart."

Black Castle

Ansel laughed at my defensive retort.

"In truth," Ansel said, "it wasn't easy for her. I saw her turmoil. I knew in my heart she loved me, but she insisted on holding me off until she completed her quest to procure a dragon egg. It turned out to be Sovann's egg. He hatched shortly after Amáne's return and linked with me. After that, she had no choice but to surrender to her feelings." He gave me a smug look. "... and to me."

I took over. "He proposed via dragonback. It was the most brilliantly romantic betrothal ever brought off."

"And she said, 'yes,' and here we are."

The room exploded with cheers, clapping and laughter.

Chapter Eight

The musicians struck up a lively tune as tables were cleared and moved to the edges of the room. Ansel led me to the center of the hall where we danced the first galliard, a courtly processional dance, which included leaps and skips in time to the music. Ansel had been helping me learn this dance for the last several weeks. He was graceful. In comparison, I was inept. I held my breath through the first few steps, hoping I wouldn't trip over my feet. The guests were invited to join us. I relaxed under Ansel's expert guidance.

The afternoon swept by. The dancing, the music, even the ballads about me, all made for a magical day.

I stood in conversation with one of the guests, Lady Eidel of Tramoren. Our discussion was interrupted by a middle-aged lord who staggered up to us, the smell of ale, like a cloud, surrounded him. His bloodshot eyes wandered from Lady Eidel to me.

"Whish of ye wenches wanna have the honor of the nex dancsh?"

"Lord Feyr!" admonished Lady Eidel. "That is no way to speak to your queen."

"Why? I happen ta know shees common-born. Same class as a ssserving girl."

BLACK CASTLE

The lady's eyes widened in shock.

I offered a reassuring smile to ease her worry, then glanced around for a dragon rider to help with the inebriated lord. I didn't think it would have been proper for a bride to wrestle down a guest. I saw Gallen already making his way over. I sighed in relief.

Before Gallen arrived, the lord grabbed my wrist. "I shoose you." Lady Eidel cried out.

I glared at the obnoxious baron and said, "Lord Feyr, kindly let go of me."

"Or wut?" He tugged me closer.

I had no choice but to deal with the situation so it wouldn't escalate before Gallen could get to me. Rotating my captured hand, I locked onto his wrist and twisted it. With my other hand, I shoved down on his elbow. He bent forward in pain.

Gallen arrived. He eyed the subdued lord and smiled.

"Remove this man from the feast," I said as I propelled him over to Gallen.

"Well done," Gallen said, and he led him away.

The crowd parted as Ansel rushed up, his eyes taking in the scene.

"Amáne?"

Adjusting my gown, I said, "It seems the good Lord Feyr attempted to drain a barrel of our DragonScale Ale single-handedly. He'll be spending the rest of the day confined to his chambers."

He put his arm protectively around me.

I turned to apologize to Lady Eidel. Her face had gone ghostly white. Attendants had rushed to her.

The lady's husband pushed his way through. "Eidel, my dear. What's going on?"

"She'll be fine," I said. "It's a wonder any of us females can breathe in the gowns into which we've been trussed."

He relaxed his concern and ushered his lady away.

At that moment, Fiona made her way to me. Concern showed on her face until she saw my smile.

Ansel turned to her. "Please tell me I can be alone with my wife before another man tries to steal her away."

Fiona laughed. "That's exactly what I've come to tell you. But, truthfully, I believe it would take more than a drunken lord to steal her away."

She led us to a corner of the hall. "The sun will be setting shortly. We've come to your final obligation, and then you may be excused." She threw a promising smile at Ansel.

"Here's the plan. There hasn't been a Drekinn dragon rider in many generations, let alone one that married another rider. This is historic. What better location to celebrate your royal wedding night than the Castle Outpost? As their gift to you, the dragon riders have created a regal wedding suite there. And I assure you, it is magnificent. This was Avano's idea. The riders and their mounts have been ousted. There will be no one but you two." She squeezed my hand in excitement.

A shiver of nerves shot through me.

"But first, Amáne," Fiona said, "I'll assist you into suitable riding clothes."

"At last," I said.

"Sovann and Eshshah are waiting for you on the south lawns," she said. "Kira, Mila and Rio will be off to the side with a basket of flower petals. Amáne, you are to walk over to them and receive the basket before you get into the saddle. Then you'll both take a short flight over the city, including the outskirts. In this way you can connect with your people. They deserve a view of their king and new queen. You'll fly low and scatter the petals throughout the city, after which your dragons will deliver you safely to the outpost. And that is where I end my responsibilities." She beamed.

"What a brilliant ending to a perfectly-planned celebration, Fiona." I hugged her tightly. "You've done an amazing job. Thank you."

"Yes, thank you Fiona." Ansel hugged her and kissed both of her cheeks.

"You are most welcome. I love you two. Now let's go change. The riders will line a path for you out of the hall." Our eyes locked. Her face glowed with emotion.

Chapter Nine

Again, Fiona created a work of art in my elaborate riding clothes. Instead of my usual tights, she'd crafted a slim gown with a split skirt. I could sit astride a saddle without anyone raising their eyebrows. And best of all — I could breathe.

She helped me don a new breastplate constructed with Eshshah's iridescent red scales. Unlike my other one, this one molded to my body in a definite feminine style and shape. The scales were left exposed in all their beauty.

A new pair of dragonscale boots completed my ensemble.

"Fiona, why didn't you let me change into this before the feast? I could have eaten so much more."

She giggled. Her hand made a circling gesture so I could turn for her appraisal. Pleased with the results, she led me back out to Ansel. His eyebrows lifted in approval.

Ansel and I walked arm-in-arm through the path of dragon riders. I smiled brightly at Avano and mouthed 'thank you.' He winked back.

The sun had just set as we exited the hall and crossed the lawn. I took in every memorable detail. Eshshah and Sovann stood

BLACK CASTLE

ahead of us. Their saddles were strung with scales from Sitara, whose name means starlight. Her scales were used in every outpost in Teravinea and in many rooms in the castle. Whispering 'Sitara' would set them glowing, lighting an area from dim to bright. The scales glimmered as we approached, adding to the enchantment.

Music filled the air. The citizens of Teravinea were lit with excitement as they jostled for a spot to catch a glimpse of us. The twenty-two dragons from the Valley of Dragons perched along the city walls, and Charna watched from the shadows.

I spotted Kira, Rio and Mila to my right. My face turned to Ansel, whose beautiful green eyes glowed as if on their own. He gazed at me with such love, I forgot to breathe. This was the happiest day of my life.

I will never forget this moment.

Departing from Ansel, I veered toward the girls for the basket of petals.

In the next breath, Eshshah let out a frightful warning roar. At once, the three girls' heads jerked up, looks of horror displayed on their faces. A shadow spread over us. My euphoria turned to terror.

Air forced from my lungs as large talons tightened around my body. I was jerked up into the sky. Pain and shock blasted through me. With another terrifying bellow, Eshshah leaped up in chase. A furious shriek along with a belching of flames shot from the large grey dragon who held me. I recoiled from the intense heat.

My captor growled in the ancient tongue.

At last I found my breath and screamed.

"Amáne, I'm with you," Eshshah said. I felt her strength flow through me. "He's told us to pull back. He said he will crush you if we come closer. We won't leave you."

I stifled a sob.

"I'm so sorry," she said. "This is the same dragon I told you about, that flew in before your ceremony. Sovann and I should have approached him straightaway. My neglect has caused this."

"Eshshah, please. Don't blame yourself. We've all been caught up in the festivities. There was no cause for any alarm at the time. We can't live on hindsight. Besides, Calder tried and couldn't find him."

"Sovann and King Ansel are keeping pace," Eshshah informed. "The dragon is only allowing me to stay near. The others must stay far behind."

"I don't understand, Eshshah. Why is he doing this?"

Eshshah conversed with the dragon, but I couldn't interpret what they said. We continued to climb. The wind whipped at me like a Valaira, the turbulent storms from my home township of Dorsal.

Eshshah had extinguished Sitara's lit scales on her saddle. I felt her presence, but could no longer see her.

"The dragon's name is Senka," Eshshah said. "He's come from the Valley of Dragons on Orchila to take you back to the island as a hostage."

"Hostage? What do the Ancient Ones want with me?"

"It's not the Ancient Ones that want you. Senka's mate is in chains. She will only be released when he delivers you to 'the Evil One.' Senka says he regrets his actions, but will do what he must for his mate."

"Orchila? That's at least a seven hour flight. Eshshah ..." I couldn't finish my thought. Fear wrapped around me.

Eshshah offered me her comfort. I felt Sovann join in, and with him, Ansel.

Pull yourself together, Amáne. There's nothing you can do at this moment.

Black Castle

I tried to take a deep breath, but Senka held me too tightly. With some effort, I held my panic in check.

"Tell Ansel I love him. We'll get out of this. I know we will."

Hanging from the huge dragon's crushing grip cut off much of my oxygen. As time passed, I drifted in and out of consciousness. Eshshah tried to convince him to give me a rest. He refused.

Each time I regained my senses, my panic and anger increased, until finally I reacted. Pounding on his claws, I shouted, "Loosen your grip! I can't breathe. Do you want to deliver me dead?"

The big grey dragon must have understood me. He relaxed his hold. But, too much. At the speed we flew, the wind tore me from his grasp. I plummeted into the darkness below.

I screamed. Eshshah shrieked. My arms flailed, grabbing at nothing. Senka dove for me and snatched me from the air with his hind claws. The jolt sent lightning pain through my body. My vision clouded, then all went black.

CHAPTER TEN

The ground lay hard and cold under me when I awoke. I inhaled and grimaced. It didn't surprise me I'd broken some ribs.

The silhouettes of Eshshah and Senka loomed overhead. They faced each other hissing and growling. Dangerously close to each other, their fangs were bared. I felt Eshshah's fear for my life as her anger increased. Senka crouched over me, keeping Eshshah from coming to my aid.

I lay helpless in the shadow of the large male's bulk. If the fight came to blows, I would be crushed. Smoke rose from Eshshah's nostrils. I'd never seen her that menacing.

Senka raised his head and trumpeted a warning.

My heart rate increased. I felt Sovann, and that meant he was close, too close.

Summoning my strength, I shouted in thought transference, "Sovann, stay your distance, circle back. We've landed."

"Amáne, are you hurt?" Sovann asked. "You screamed."

"Just stay away, please." Relief spread over me as I felt the distance between us increase, until I felt his presence no more.

Black Castle

The ground shook with the thunder-like growl that echoed in Eshshah's chest. Heedless that the grey dragon was so much larger, she would not back down.

Senka exhaled and turned his head from her in apparent defeat. Taking care to not trample me, he retreated. I sang a silent song of thanks.

Eshshah kept her whirling eyes on the large grey and stepped toward me. As soon as he put some distance between us, my dragon lowered her head. I felt her healing breath. At first, a tingle, and then intense heat radiated as my ribs began to mend. When Eshshah pulled back, I inhaled deeply.

I sat up slowly, took her fangs in my hands and pulled her face to mine. Leaning my forehead on her nose, I closed my eyes and hummed to her, comforting both of us.

"I don't know what this is all about. There has to be some mistake, here. I'm sure everything will be fine. Let Sovann and Ansel know we're all right."

Senka growled something to Eshshah. My dragon snapped at him.

"He is impatient to return to the air." She drew her head back down to me, and said, "I convinced him to let you put my saddle on him."

"That's a brilliant idea." I rose cautiously, testing my condition. Eshshah had the most remarkable healing powers of any dragon. My ribs had healed completely.

Before removing the saddle from Eshshah, I pulled off my ring and Queen Fiala's priceless jewelry and stashed them in a small compartment in the side of the saddle. Not sure of where the saddle would end up, I thought my jewels would still fare better there than on me. I gathered my strength and threw the saddle up onto Senka.

Securing it, however, proved to be quite a challenge. Made for Eshshah, the cinch barely reached around the larger dragon's girth.

"Exhale, Senka, you're not making this any easier for me. I can't buckle it if you continue to take such deep breaths. And keep still."

I ignored his angry retort. Even though he spoke in the ancient tongue, it wasn't too difficult to guess his message.

Double-checking my work, I tested the buckles before I mounted. Reaching the saddle took a couple tries. He was even larger than Sovann. Once astride, I secured myself into the footpegs, thankful he waited until I was safely fastened before he launched.

The force of Senka's takeoff gave me a painful jolt. I should have expected it, since chances were he'd never carried a rider. Eshshah and I had flown together so long, we were practically one in takeoff and in flight. Our flights began with a smooth leap into the air, and I was accustomed to her style. Once I recovered and learned Senka's rhythm, I eventually relaxed in the saddle.

About three hours before dawn, Eshshah roused me from my stupor. The island of Orchila lay ahead. Moonlight shone off the white sand beaches that surrounded the tropical emerald island.

"Eshshah, tell Sovann to veer to the west, to the beach where you waited for me on our previous trip. They can land there and you can stay in contact."

On our last visit to Orchila, we'd arrived on the southwestern shore. I'd left Eshshah there while I made my way into the small port town. My ill-fated adventure began there. We'd intended only a short trip to procure a map showing us the way to the Valley of Dragons. Instead I'd been sold out as a sacrifice to save a local tribe.

Senka stayed on his current path, heading to the north of the island.

Black Castle

Eshshah dropped low to just above the tree tops so she wouldn't be in the line of sight of anyone tracking the night sky. I caught a view of the north shore. The waves broke over the sand and lit up as if by their own luminescence. The jungle grew almost down to the water, leaving only a strip of white sand. A cone-shaped form rose to the west. I'd read about those mountains that held an inferno in their depths. When their pressure built, they erupted in molten rock.

As we descended, I could make out a clearing, like an ugly black scar in the midst of the dense jungle. The clearing was set a small distance south from the north shore. I focused on the dark patch.

We approached quickly. A black castle came into view, partially in ruins. The sinister-looking stronghold had blended into the darkness of the clearing and was upon us before I realized what it was. Its spires twisted like deadly vines silhouetting against the green backdrop. Built from the black rock of the volcano, the fortress reared up from the dark scarred earth. The back north section lay toppled and appeared to almost melt into the hardened lava flow that had reclaimed a portion of the stronghold. The front looked like it had survived a violent mountain eruption. Building equipment took up the area around the ruined section, restoration under way.

Who would set up a fortress in the path of a lava flow? And why would someone choose to rebuild it?

Senka began his spiraling descent. My heart quickened. My body shook. The purpose of my capture would soon be evident.

"Eshshah," I whispered out loud.

"I'm with you Amáne." Her calming strength filled me.

I watched below as torches were lit and men scrambled across the south-facing courtyard. Soldiers were posted on the battlements.

I caught the actions of bowstrings being drawn. Blades glinted the torchlight.

A groan issued from Senka. I followed the direction of his gaze and my heart sank. In the middle of the courtyard lay a large yellow dragon. Chains covered her like a spider's web. Not one of her limbs could move more than an arm's length — my arm's length. An iron collar surrounded the dragon's neck, just behind her head. Even from where I observed, it was too tight to allow her to swallow anything large enough to fully nourish her. An unhealthy number of her scales were scattered on the ground.

Flames of anger overcame my fear. The moment Senka touched ground, I slid from the saddle. Crossbows were brought up as the soldiers rushed toward me. Some aimed at Senka, others at the yellow dragon and a few at me.

"Halt there," a rough-looking man yelled.

"Why am I here?" I turned on the man. "Who's ordered my capture?"

"Amáne," Eshshah warned.

I spun in a full circle, searching for the person responsible for my capture. Only soldiers were present, and possibly a captain. If that someone didn't want me alive, then I would already be with my ancestors. The thought gave me a sense of boldness. Keeping my eyes focused on the defeated dragon, I moved in her direction. I put out calming thoughts and exuded a sense of sympathy that I knew she could feel.

"I said halt, or we will shoot!" the man commanded.

Only when I faced Senka's mate did I halt. I felt the dragon's pain and terror, but also her trust. Senka's suffering wrenched my heart.

I wheeled around and faced the men surrounding me, their crossbows close enough to go right through me, should they choose to fire — or fire by mistake. I noted many kept their eyes on the dragon, their fear reflecting overtly.

"I've been delivered," I shouted at the soldiers. "Senka has done what he was coerced to do. Now let his mate go. Unchain her." I doubted she even had the strength to fly.

"Now, if that isn't a sight that would make the next legendary ballad ..."

A chill went up my spine at the sound of the oily voice that filled my ears.

"'The Girl of the Prophecy That Destroyed a Reign Goes on to Save a Captured Dragon.' I'll instruct my musicians to come up with something befitting your fame."

I swung my eyes to my right. On a second-story balcony a dark silhouette stood against the light that spilled from behind him. Galtero. The man who had sent Ansel's parents to their ancestors. The same man who, though he didn't wield the blade, was responsible for slitting my father's throat.

Bile – and fear – rose from my stomach. I forced a swallow.

"Chain the girl. Take her to the tower. I'm going back to bed."

CHAPTER ELEVEN

I sat with my back against the cold stone and surveyed my round cell. Tilting my head back, I stared at the partially-restored ceiling high above. Three small windows, barred and too far out of reach, let in the first light of dawn. The irons around my wrists and ankles cut into my skin.

"Oh Ansel," I moaned to myself. A tear slid down my cheek. I lifted my chained hands and wiped it away with the back of my arm.

Was it just the day before I danced, laughed and kissed my new husband? Our wedding night over and only a handful of kisses had passed between us.

My head jerked in the direction of the door as a key slid into the lock. Hinges creaked and it flung open. My cell filled with six men, fully armed.

I raised an eyebrow and couldn't stop myself from saying, "All six of you just to fetch me?"

"No talking. We won't be bewitched by you."

"Bewitched? What did he tell you of me?"

"Silence!" The man bent over and took a swing at me. I ducked.

He raised his hand again.

"Stand back," said the head guard, coming between the first man and me. He yanked me to my feet by my chains. I winced and rubbed the raw skin under the irons. With teeth clenched, I glared.

One of the guards leered at me. His greasy hair hung down to his shoulders and into his pockmarked face. I wondered if he'd ever visited a bathing room in his life.

"Maybe y'are possessed but yer a pretty little thing up close, yeah," he said.

He reached out and ran his finger along my face and down to my collar bone. I turned my head and leaned away.

"I like my women with a little more weight on their bones, uh huh," he continued. "With somethin' to 'em, y'understand? But yer not half bad." His eyes raked my body up and down.

My heart pounded against my ribs. His captain watched on, amused.

Where is their sense of honor? I huffed at my own question. *They have no honor.*

The odious man grasped my face and brought his closer. "Mmm, an' ya smell good, too. I bet ya taste just as good." He leaned in.

Hot anger seized my fear.

"Eshshah."

"I'm with you, Amáne."

Her strength poured into me. I ducked my chin and head-butted the knave. His close proximity didn't give me the full advantage and force, but it was enough to stop his advance. He cried out and grabbed his face. Blood gushed from his nose.

My jaw flashed with pain as his fist slammed into me. I stumbled backwards into the arms of another guard.

The men burst into laughter.

"Aww, Gahn, you got a lot ta learn about how to get what ya want from a woman. Let me show ya how it's done."

The man who'd caught me, tightened his arms around me and brought his face down to my neck.

"Yer, right, she does smell g —"

I arched my back, rammed the back of my head into his chin, scraped my foot down his shin and stomped on his foot.

He released me. I spun around and held my chained hands in front of me in a defensive stance. A futile act, maybe, seeing the six armed men before me, but I was ready to draw more blood. With Eshshah's help I stood a chance — a small one, perhaps, but a chance nonetheless.

"That's enough," said the captain. "Galtero won't take kindly to damage done to his valuables. You had your fun, boys. It looks like her answer is, 'no,' for now."

Without another word, they dragged me out of my cell. Three men preceded me and three took up the rear. I noted the greasy one tried to position himself close, but was blocked by another who took up behind me.

The stairs out of the tower were narrow. We went single file as we snaked our way down. I peered out of an arrowslit and noticed we'd reached ground level, but we kept descending.

They ushered me through several turns down a confusing maze of corridors. We arrived at a set of large wooden double-doors.

My guards shoved at the heavy portal, which opened up to a lengthy chamber. It gave all the appearances of a throne room. There, Galtero ensconced himself in a high-back chair, both hands rested on the carved arms, a superior smirk on his ugly face. He wore a crown and acted every bit the king.

Black Castle

King of what?

The soldiers led me down the long plush carpet woven with images of phantasmagorical landscapes and creatures. They stopped me several paces in front of a narrow table that stood before Galtero's chair.

A door to his right opened and a tall woman, hauntingly beautiful, glided out. She came to a halt beside Galtero, placing her hand over his. I couldn't judge her age, but she was much younger than him. Even young enough to be his daughter. Her alabaster skin, nearly translucent, accentuated her striking features. The lady's painted red lips stood out in sharp contrast against her pale complexion. The thought of why this beautiful lady wanted to be with him turned my stomach.

I revised my initial impression of beauty when I met her eyes. Looking into them was like gazing into a ghastly dark pit. I thought Galtero had a malevolent glare, but hers put a chill up my spine. If poison were personified, it would be she.

Over her black gown, the lady wore a dark cape lined in red, and on her head was a circlet with a ruby that hung on her forehead. The vision of a black widow came to mind.

Minutes passed as Galtero took his time to study me. His scowl deepened, his lip curled up on one side. The woman eyed me with disdain.

I called on Eshshah for mental strength to bare their scrutiny without loosing my tongue.

"I'm with you, Amáne," Eshshah responded. "Please take care. Don't say anything rash."

After a heavy sigh, Galtero broke his silence. "You're just a little girl. You don't look like much up close, for as much grief as you've caused me," he hissed. "All the more reason why I burn to send you to your ancestors. I swore if I ever had the occasion to endure your presence again, I would end your despicable life." His voice was nasal and he held his S's.

A snake and a black widow. My present company couldn't be more malicious.

I remained silent.

He rose from his seat and moved around to the front of the table. That's when I noticed his left arm hung limp at his side. My memory flew back to our last meeting when I thought he'd killed Eshshah. I'd gone berserk and cut down all his men to get to him. The coward had been astride a horse, which he wheeled around to escape my wrath. In desperation I'd hurled my glaive, at his back as he retreated. Although I aimed for his black heart, my blade found purchase in his shoulder.

I couldn't hide my smirk as I realized his useless arm was to my credit.

"I see my injury amuses you." His eyes became slits. If he could have dispatched me with only his glare, this would have been the moment.

Reaching behind his back with his good arm, Galtero drew a wicked-looking dagger. He flourished it in front of my face, coming so close, I felt the air move. I tried to hold my gaze steady, but couldn't help but blink when his knife neared my eyes.

I swallowed. Out of the corner of my eye, I saw the red lips of the lady curve up in a gratifying smile.

Galtero's display over, he held his dagger vertically between his face and mine. With the thumb of the same hand, he ran it along the blade, testing its edge.

A drop of red formed on his thumb. He examined it and then slowly licked the blood from his finger.

BLACK CASTLE

I nearly retched.

The villain's eyes focused on mine. He turned his wrist and pressed the blade to my neck. My blood froze.

"Yes, I fantasized about all of the ways I would finish you — to pay you back." He licked his lips.

I turned my turned my head away in disgust and suppressed a shudder. Clenching my teeth, I pulled my eyes back to his face.

"But," he said, pulling the knife away. He paused as he admired his reflection in the polished metal. "Unfortunately you are more valuable alive. Especially now that you are the Queen Consort of Teravinea."

He barked a sharp laugh, ending in a hiss. "Oh, go ahead and glare at me little girl. Glare all you like. Aren't you going to ask me how I could be so generous as to spare your life?"

As curious as I was, I would not give him the satisfaction he craved. I kept my eyes on his, and didn't lower my gaze. I could tell this irritated him.

His lady crossed her arms and let out a long slow breath. The passage of air through her throat created a rushing-ocean sound. I felt her eyes on me even as mine didn't leave Galtero's.

He went on as if I had asked. "I am going to test your new husband to find out if he thinks you're worth ransoming. Are you dear enough to him to trade you for a dragon egg?"

"A dragon egg?" I couldn't help saying.

I'd let Eshshah in on our conversation via open thought transference. She shared the events through my eyes. "Doesn't he know a human doesn't choose the dragon, the dragon chooses their rider?" she said.

"You can't do anything with a dragon egg. Are you that ignorant?" I blurted out.

The head guard, who stood to my right, backhanded me so hard, my sight darkened. I would have fallen if they hadn't held so tightly to my chains.

"You don't talk to the king like that!" my assailant said.

How could they still think he's the king?

Galtero snickered. "No, I believe you are the ignorant one. Of course I know that old myth about how a dragon will hatch only for its Chosen One. But that no longer holds true." His eyes swung toward the lady. A smug look passed between them. "Lady Ravana can bend the will of the weak little dragon to choose me for its rider."

She's a sorceress.

"I will become immortal."

I flinched at his grin. "Dragon riders are not immortal."

"Oh, I am aware of that, child. You may not have noticed, but I am along in my years. As a dragon rider, with dragon venom running in my veins, I will live another one or two hundred years. That would be sufficient immortality to accomplish what I need."

Anger sent heat rising up my neck. "If you succeed in forcing a dragon, I hope he uses the full measure of his venom when his fangs sink into you in the linking."

I felt Eshshah groan.

Before I could duck, a guard slammed the palm of his hand into the side of my head. Stars exploded before my eyes.

The black widow let out a low laugh.

Galtero kept his eyes on me and waited for me to recover from the blow before he continued. "I assume your faithful creature has followed you here?"

I didn't respond.

Black Castle

"You'd better hope it won't do anything stupid. That would only assure your demise. And, I wager your beloved husband had to stay behind? His duty to the kingdom and all that rubbish." He made a swiping motion with his dagger.

I stood silent.

He paced back and forth in front of me, his eyes never ceased their inspection. As he moved, his left arm swung uselessly.

I pressed my lips together, my eyes narrowed.

Galtero tipped his head. "Your non-response is as good as answering. You haven't yet mastered deception, girl. Your mate did not accompany you, and your dragon did. I thought that much. It will enable negotiations to proceed at a quicker pace. He can take my proposal back to Teravinea."

"She. Eshshah's a she. And I won't take part in enslaving a hatching dragon," I said.

The man who'd hit me jerked his head in my direction, but didn't strike me again.

"I don't care what gender it is, you don't have a choice, my dear. Negotiations will begin immediately. Your betrothed, I'm sure, is anxiously waiting to hear from you. Safe at home in his castle, longing to get you back into his arms. Newlyweds." He made it sound like a curse. "I'm sure he's not yet tasted enough of your passion."

I dropped my eyes.

Galtero stopped in front of me, a shark catching scent of his prey. Bending forward, he brought his face closer to mine. He grabbed my chin and lifted. The stench of his rotting teeth couldn't be masked by the mint leaves he chewed.

If he tries to kiss me, I'll bite him.

"Amáne, please control yourself," Eshshah urged. "I fear for your safety. Don't antagonize him."

Trying to hide my fear, I raised my eyes to meet Galtero's. I caught him studying my attire. His eyebrows lifted.

"What? Do I detect you have not, as yet, seen a sunrise with your husband? Were you taken directly from your ceremony?" A glint of black pleasure reflected in his eyes.

Ravana barked out a rude laugh.

Flinching involuntarily, I squeezed my stinging eyes shut before they filled.

Wicked laughter echoed in the room. It sent my heart to my throat.

"All the more urgency on Drekinn's part," Galtero said. "He will make the right decision. Whether he wants you back piece by piece or relatively whole."

My stomach twisted. Wrestling for control, I opened my eyes. Galtero's evil ones pierced mine. He turned and strode to the end of the table, then spun and faced me. His useless arm continued its momentum like a pendulum before it slowed to a stop.

A corner of his mouth turned up. "Oh, I do believe he would prefer his bride intact."

I called again upon Eshshah in thought transference.

"I'm with you, Amáne."

Her strength filled me. It gave me courage to face whatever Galtero had in mind.

"Bring her forward," he commanded.

The men jerked my bindings, pulling me close to where Galtero stood. I thrashed and struggled. A brief sense of satisfaction washed over me as I noticed how they had to strain to drag me to the tyrant.

Six men.

"Thank you, Eshshah."

BLACK CASTLE

The guards forced me forward until I was pushed up to the edge of the table.

Ravana slid in beside Galtero, a disturbing anticipation written on her face.

"Her hand," he ordered.

The head guard grabbed my left hand. I resisted with all my might, and Eshshah's. Two more men joined in to assist him. My captors forced my hand flat on the table. Bile rose in my throat as Galtero tested the keenness of his black dagger on his sleeve. Its perfect edge sliced through the fabric.

"Your king will know how inflexible I am. Your life for a dragon egg." He smirked, then continued in his oily snake-like voice, "Just a small token of my seriousness. It's not much — this time. You should be thankful I will not be taking your entire arm. That would actually satisfy me as an even trade." His eyes darted to his lifeless arm. "If Ansel Drekinn does not grasp the weight of my demand, then I will be happy to show him larger proof."

I bit back a scream as his blade hovered over my end finger.

The lady leaned in. Her tongue passed lightly over her lips. A spider anticipating the trouncing of her prey.

Galtero jutted his face into mine. His vile breath nearly made me gag. "Now, you can make this easy and fast, or, if you continue to fight it, believe me I will take delight in cutting slowly through the joint, sawing at the tendon, taking all the time I want. Either way, I will have the proof I need to send a meaningful message."

I shot him my most defiant glare, clenched my jaw and held my hand immobile on the table.

My lips pressed together as I called silently to Eshshah.

Galtero bore down on his blade and sliced it through the first joint of my little finger. Eshshah suffered with me.

Having obtained the 'token of his seriousness,' he handed me a rag and said, "Don't bleed on my rugs."

I couldn't help but be angry at myself for the tears that escaped as I wrapped his dirty cloth around my mutilated finger and pressed it to my chest. I didn't look at Galtero or Ravana, but had no doubt they found pleasure in my pain. Eshshah gently reprimanded me for my self-reproach, but I considered my tears a failure in self control, a show of weakness.

A small wooden box, with long leather straps attached, was brought to Galtero. In it he placed the piece of my finger and a sealed parchment.

"Now, girl," he said, "call to your dragon. I know it is close and can hear you. Tell it to land near the west wall. It must allow this to be strapped to its leg." He held up the grotesque box. "The message will be taken back to Teravinea. I know Ansel Drekinn will follow the instructions enclosed. I will give the dragon three days to return with an egg. Plenty of time. You'd best appreciate my generosity."

He brought his eyebrows together and said, "You make sure your dragon understands he will take no action against my men, or his next delivery will be your entire arm, or perhaps your head. Make certain he heeds my words."

"I told you before, Eshshah is a female."

The head guard backhanded me.

CHAPTER TWELVE

My captors escorted me from Galtero's throne room. I paid sharp attention to the route we took.

"Amáne," Eshshah said, "let's hope they deliver you back to the tower. It would be the most accessible part of the castle. I believe it should be possible to reach you there once darkness falls."

Hope threw its light on my desperation.

To Eshshah's and my disappointment, they didn't bring me back to the tower, but to a different cell. They led me into a tiny room. The guards turned and filed out, the last being the vulgar man who'd harassed me earlier. He puckered his lips at me and exhaled a lascivious laugh before he turned and strode out of the room. The lock clicked in place.

A quick survey of my new cell told me it would have been used as a storage closet at one time. Wooden bowls and tankards filled the shelves that lined the walls. All useless to me.

Eight strides made up its length, and maybe three wide. I paced the room, holding my injured finger tightly. Closing my eyes, I summoned my powers. After linking with Eshshah, I had acquired some of her healing gift. Relief spread as my hands heated. The severed end of my finger began to mend.

Healing always took a toll on my strength, but my skills had improved. I knew when to stop before I became light-headed. I also had to consider if anyone happened to check my finger, I didn't want to raise any suspicions. I quit before the damage was completely repaired, then rewrapped it with the bloody rag. My powers did not include regeneration. I would always have part of my finger missing. My only hope was that more of me won't be lost before this ordeal ended.

"Eshshah, before you deliver that box to Ansel, could you please ask Sovann to get a message to him?"

"Of course, Amáne. Sovann told me King Ansel's been asking about you. He's overwrought with worry."

I closed my eyes and pictured Ansel. The thought of him suffering on my account proved almost worse than what I just went through.

"Please tell him I'm alright, but I need him to know what Galtero just did. I think if we tell him what is about to be delivered, it would go easier for him."

"I believe you're right," Eshshah said.

I waited while the message was conveyed to Ansel, through Sovann. My tears welled up.

"Amáne, I explained to Sovann as gently as I could what King Ansel will be receiving. There's no easy way to prepare for that. The king promises you'll be out soon. They're working on a plan. Avano, Braonán and the other riders are making trips back to Teravinea to bring supplies and troops. There's not enough time to transport many, but he'll make good use of the soldiers they bring. He said to tell you a local merchant has allowed us to use a building of his, outside of the village. It had been an inn at one time, built to accommodate dragons."

"Please tell him that gives me a lot of hope."

"King Ansel was pleased to hear Galtero believes he is still in Teravinea. It'll buy us some time. He said he may send one of the other riders to choose an egg. He didn't want me to leave you. I wouldn't have wanted to, either."

"Eshshah, he can't actually be thinking of bringing Galtero an egg?"

I waited for his response through our dragons.

"The king hopes an egg won't be necessary. But as a last resort, he'll do what he must to get you back."

"Tell him I can't be responsible for enslaving a dragon."

I paced the tiny cell as our conversation went back and forth through Eshshah and Sovann.

"He said he can't be responsible for the loss of his queen, his love, his wife. Truthfully, Amáne, I agree with him. I too will do what must be done to get you out of there."

The day dragged on. The temperature in the enclosed cell increased to sweltering proportions. Sweat ran down my forehead and burned my eyes. My mouth and throat became dry as my thirst increased. This was a tropical island. Buildings constructed of bamboo and thatched roofs made up the norm in architecture, not an airless castle of lava rock.

Who built this place? Probably a tyrant like Galtero who didn't know anything about the tropics.

The turnkey visited only once. He brought a bowl of a purple mush-like porridge and a small cup of water. The porridge was made from the underground stems of a local plant. I gagged it down. The small amount of water hardly quenched my thirst.

I dozed on and off for an interminable amount of time. The noise of the door opening startled me awake. Several heavily-armed men yanked me out of the cell and pushed me through another series of confusing corridors. I noted with relief, the greasy-haired man was not among this group. Judging by the light filtering down from the windows high above, it was probably midday. The closet had been so dark, I didn't realize the night had passed.

The men ushered me into a dining chamber where Galtero sat at the head of a heavy table. His sorceress occupied a chair to his right. Two large plates of juicy roasted meat with vegetables steaming in bowls sat before them. I inhaled the aroma. If I weren't dehydrated, my mouth would have watered.

The head guard shoved me down into a seat across from the two. He secured my wrists to the arms of the chair, my feet to its legs. After they bowed to the despot, the guards left. I was certain they were not far away, should Galtero need to summon them.

I swallowed, staring at the food across the table.

Galtero picked up his dagger, the same one he'd used to cut off my finger. A twinge coursed through my hand. He turned the dagger in different angles in front of his face, studying its edge.

As I watched his movements, knowing they were meant to provoke, I concentrated on my breathing, slowing the beating of my heart. Galtero's eyes narrowed as I held his gaze. I refused to squirm or make known my fear. His jaw tightened.

"Eshshah," I called in thought transference.

"You're doing well, Amáne. Hold your anger."

Galtero exhaled audibly before turning his attention to his meal. He directed the blade to his plate and began to slowly slice a piece of meat, using his one good hand. Stabbing a bite, he made

BLACK CASTLE

a show of putting it in his mouth and chewing. He put his knife down, grabbed a golden goblet and took a noisy gulp, then burped. I pressed my lips together in disgust. Focusing on a spot on the table in front of me, I forced my countenance into a neutral expression. I felt Galtero's eyes boring into me. He sliced another piece of meat and repeated his previous sequence, chewing with the manners of a pig. I couldn't muffle the sound of my stomach as it called out for a share.

All the while, Ravana took dainty bites from her plate, also making a show of enjoying her meal.

Galtero taunted me with his third mouthful, and said, "Don't get the idea I invited you here to idly watch me dine."

Invited? I'd hardly call this an invitation.

"I'm going to make good use of your time while I await my dragon egg."

My eyes raised to his. My brows furrowed.

A wicked smile twisted his face. He spoke around the food still in his mouth, "You will instruct me."

My chest constricted in anger. I opened my mouth to respond.

"Amáne," Eshshah entreated.

"Thank you, Eshshah. I'll control my tongue."

With a deep breath, I gathered myself, then exhaled. "Instruct you?" I said in an even tone.

"You will tell me all I need to know about linking with a dragon. I want to know how long the hatching takes. What the dragon does first. If the dragon bite is painful. If so, what have they found that will alleviate the pain? How long before I can fly on it — I want to know everything."

My nostrils flared.

Before I could respond, Galtero shouted over his shoulder, "Girl, bring me more wine."

A young native girl carried out a pitcher. I noted the hobbles on her ankles. She wore a sarong-type garment that wrapped around her body and tied behind her neck. Her hair fell forward, veiling her face.

As she bent to fill both Ravana's and Galtero's goblets, I got a better look.

Impossible!

It was Lia'ina, the daughter of a chief from a local tribe. The same tribe that, some time ago, intended to use me as a human sacrifice to the Ancient Ones in the Valley of Dragons.

How is it that she has become a serving girl?

Her eyes caught mine and opened wide. I gave a minute shake of my head, and was relieved to see her quickly mask her shock. Even though the circumstances of our last encounter were quite traumatic for me, I held no animosity toward her.

Galtero dismissed Lia'ina with a wave of his hand. She backed away and disappeared through a door.

The self-appointed king turned back to me after a noisy slurp of his wine.

"Now, begin. What is first thing that happens when a dragon hatches?"

I remained silent.

"If you value the next joint of your finger, you - will - talk." He shook his blade at me in time to his last three words.

"Amáne," Eshshah said. "No harm will be done by telling him some simple facts. Much of the linking rite is common knowledge, anyway. Please make this easier on yourself."

Eshshah was right, as usual. Reluctantly, I told Galtero how a dragon egg starts to vibrate and hum as it draws in its Chosen One. I didn't get far in my narrative, when one of his men rushed in and whispered in his ear. I caught something about a dragon.

Black Castle

Galtero raised an eyebrow and called out, "Guards! Quickly. Come take the dragon rider. Take her to the old kitchen in the abandoned wing."

He snickered at me. "Don't be thinking you will be held in the same cell twice. Escape will not be within your grasp, this time."

I was led through the partially-destroyed section of the castle I'd seen from the air. The guards shoved me into a large room that at one time must have been a busy kitchen. The hearth lay cold and unused. A layer of dust blanketed the tables that still stood. The other furniture in the room had given in to wood rot and wood-boring insects. Part of the roof and the top of the far wall were missing. The heavy tropical air replaced the dead air of the lower levels. Although, still stifling, it was an improvement.

My chains were secured to a metal structure that had once been used to hold a spit. The men inspected my irons, vigorously yanking at them, testing their strength before they rushed from the room.

I tried to think of a reason Galtero dismissed me so quickly. Something was amiss.

Maybe Ansel is on his way?

I reached out to Eshshah to ask her, when I heard a swish. A shadow passed the doorway. Someone was making an effort to approach undetected. My constraints wouldn't allow much freedom, but I tensed to defend myself as best I could.

Barely audible footsteps crept slowly toward me. My sight was blocked by a brick oven to my right. The intruder stopped and waited behind the oven.

I held my breath and called for Eshshah's strength, my ears attuned to the shallow breathing of my visitor.

"Show yourself," I said.

A small gasp echoed nearby.

"Amáne, it Lia'ina." The native girl poked her head from her hiding place, her fingers to her lips, eyes wide with fear. Crouching, she moved toward me, glancing left and right for anyone who may have heard me call out.

"Please, eat." She held out a small loaf of bread in which she'd stuffed a piece of meat.

I grabbed the offering from her and devoured it as she watched. She pulled a flask from a pouch at her side and handed it to me. Water had never tasted so good.

Tucking the empty flask back in her pouch, Lia'ina took my chained hands in hers and brought them to her forehead. She shook her head at the metal bands surrounding my wrists. With tears welling in her eyes she said, "Lia'ina want help Amáne leave this place. One time you prisoner at my tribe. I have shame of that time. I ask Amáne forgive."

"Of course I forgive you, Lia'ina. But you're as much a prisoner here, as I. How do you expect to help me if you aren't even free?"

"I not know. I think and think. Lia'ina owe Amáne."

"You don't owe me. My captivity by your tribe was not of your doing. That's in the past, now. You're brave to even be here, Lia'ina. I don't want you to get hurt on account of me. My dragon and my friends — and my husband — are going to get me out of here. When they do, we'll take you with us."

"Husband? Amáne have husband?"

"Barely. I was snatched from my wedding." My lip trembled.

The native girl gave a quick squeeze to my hands before releasing them.

"Lia'ina help. No matter ropes on feet." She gestured to her hobbles.

BLACK CASTLE

Her eyes lit up. She tapped her head. "Lia'ina think idea. Every day Lia'ina walk to meet man. He name Manu'eno. He bring food for castle. Supply come by cart and animal. Not know name of animal. Like horse, but small. Galtero demand many thing, many food. Manu'eno come each day with cart. Lia'ina tell Manu'eno. Him help Amáne. He know my father before ... before ..."

Lia'ina took in a long breath and swallowed hard. I held no love for her father, the tribal chief. I knew Lia'ina had been a good and obedient daughter, and as such, she would have a daughter's respect for him.

"I'm sorry for you if something has happened to your father," I said.

"All my family, my tribe, no more. Galtero capture for slave, or send to ancestors. Lia'ina promise to avenge." She closed her hands into fists and shook them.

Bootsteps sounded from the hallway. Lia'ina glanced around in alarm, then gave me an encouraging nod before she disappeared behind the oven.

Shouts and panicked voices echoed outside the kitchen. From the ruined walls of my confinement I could see a small portion of the battlements to the west. Trees blocked most of my view, but men with crossbows were visible as they mustered along the wall-walk.

A chilling screech resonated from the sky, a keening that raised the hair on the nape of my neck. It came from a dragon.

"Eshshah! What's going on out there?"

"It's Senka. His mate just ... He is keening for her loss. He's taken flight and is heading toward the castle. I'm going to follow."

Senka's shrieking sent my heart to my throat. I couldn't block his cries of desperation nor the sounds of terror that came from the men on the walls. Orders were shouted, but it seemed like nothing but chaos echoed from the heights.

"Amáne, he's attacking. They have harpoon cannons. He doesn't stand a chance alone. I must go help him."

"No, Eshshah. Please. I'm sorry, but I need you."

A flash of fire lit up the grounds just outside the kitchen. The temperature rose as Senka belched an inferno at Galtero's soldiers. Stones from the kitchen walls crashed down. A choking dust filled the room.

"Amáne, if I don't stop him, you'll be crushed in the fray, or burned in his flames."

"I'm all right, Eshshah. The outer walls should be far enough from me." I coughed. "Please don't come closer."

Eshshah remained at a distance and shared her view in open thought transference.

Through her eyes I saw Senka dive in for another assault. Scores of men burst into flame. Their screams filled the air.

The stench of burning flesh reached my sensitive nose. Heat from Senka's wrath could be felt through the broken roof and dilapidated walls.

Circling the castle, the fierce grey dragon trumpeted in anger. Swooping low, he plucked men from the wall walk and tossed them like rubbish to their deaths below. He disregarded the arrows that filled the sky.

Senka's fire continued to rain down upon Galtero's men. A harpoon cannon went off. He dodged it. The missile flew harmlessly past him.

Enraged, he came in for a strike. The boom from another cannon shook the walls. More rocks and dust fell into the kitchen.

BLACK CASTLE

A piercing screech assaulted my ears. I felt Eshshah's shock and sorrow and I saw what she saw — Senka fell from the sky.

The grounds became silent except for a few orders shouted on the battlements.

Anger swirled in my chest, matching that of Eshshah's. My heart beat violently.

"Oh Eshshah." I squeezed my eyes shut. "Two more dragons dead because of Galtero. I can't be a part of him becoming a dragon rider. Please get a message to Ansel immediately. He has to know about this."

I wiped my eyes with the back of my sleeve as I waited for Eshshah to speak to Sovann. He would convey the events to Ansel.

"Amáne," she said, "King Ansel is as outraged as we are. Sovann told me it's getting more difficult to keep his rider from storming the castle."

"Poor Ansel. I pray he has better sense than that."

"Sovann and the riders will keep a close eye on him. They won't allow him any foolishness. Plans are being made. He said to assure you he will see you soon."

"Please tell him he can't bring a dragon egg here. I don't want one even close to Galtero. I'll take no chances."

After a pause, Eshshah responded, "He insists it will only be a back-up plan, but he'll use it as a ruse. King Ansel has no intention of actually letting Galtero have an egg, but he'll do what he needs to get you back."

I could understand his position. I would do the same, but I repeated that Galtero must in no way get his hands on a dragon egg.

"Eshshah, I have news that might help a dragon rider or two get into the castle. Ask Ansel if he remembers the native girl I told him about, Lia'ina. Tell him she's here. She's a prisoner, too.

There's a man she meets every day, someone she knows, who delivers foodstuff to the castle. He frequents a place in the village called the Tavern of the Ancient Ones. His name is Manu'eno. She told me she'll connect him with —"

The sound of men approaching broke into our conversation.

"Someone's coming. Please tell Ansel about Manu'eno. And tell him I love him. I'll be with him soon. I'm sure of it."

My now-familiar guards stomped in. The head guard unlocked my chains from the spit and jerked me toward a kitchen exit.

The greasy-haired man was part of the group this time. He situated himself to my right, close enough I could smell his breath. Every few minutes he would reach out and stroke my hair or my arm. My skin crawled at his touch.

They led me through another series of corridors. It seemed Galtero not only changed the location of my cells, he never received me in the same room, either.

Paranoid weakling.

I gasped as the door opened onto a small replica of the hatching grounds of Castle Teravinea. An oval room with a sand floor spread out before me. A few tiers of wooden benches curved around above, taking up about a third of the chamber.

Galtero sat in the front row and looked down at me as I stood on the sand, a sickening leer on his face. A scribe sat to his left with a quill and ink, his hand poised above a journal. Ravana took her place to his right.

"Now, let us take up where we left off, before the interruption," he said in his nasally voice.

"You've killed two more dragons!"

"That is none of your concern. Begin. Tell me of the hatching."

"You've murdered dragons! Here. Now." The hysteria rose in my voice.

Black Castle

Before I lost control, I inhaled slowly. My temper had been the bane of my life, and had never served me well. Galtero would just feed off of my frantic ranting. However, I couldn't let the subject drop.

In a calm, yet strong voice, I said, "How, if I may ask, can you expect to be a dragon rider with the blood of so many dragons on your hands?"

"I do not need to answer your ill-mannered questions. But, to demonstrate my hospitality, I will answer you — this one time only. Your next outburst may cost you."

He paused and glared at me, eyebrows raised as if to verify I understood.

"The she-dragon died of her weakness, and her mate attacked my castle. It was rightfully defended. I will do what is necessary."

"I will not be a part of this."

"You have little choice if you value your life, girl."

"Well, maybe my life is not worth the life of another dragon."

Eshshah echoed her version of a gasp.

"Enough!" Galtero bellowed. "You will instruct me. Now. You are wasting my time." He drew his knife and made a cutting motion, simulating the severing of another joint in my finger.

My anger pushed aside the fear of his knife. "You want to learn what it's like to link with a dragon?" I said through gritted teeth. "Very well. Listen carefully."

I paused, making sure I had his full attention. "Once the hatchling breaks from its shell, it will hypnotize you with its swirling, glowing eyes. Draw you in. Lure you toward itself. You won't be in control of your actions. You will have no choice but to move closer to the dragon. So close, you can see his sharp white fangs. Possibly even see the venom dripping from the tips."

I drew a secret pleasure seeing Galtero's eyes go wide.

He opened his mouth to say something, but I continued. "Once you are near enough, the dragon will strike." I mimicked the motion with my hand. Galtero jumped. "He will bury his razor-edged poisonous fangs deep into the flesh of your right shoulder. The venom he pumps into your body will feel like hot lava in your veins. You will never have felt such excruciating pain in your life. The fire will travel up to your head so it feels like it would explode, and then burn down to the tips of your toes. Every muscle, every organ will scream in agony. Your eyes will bulge, your throat may close. To answer your earlier question, there is nothing that will relieve your pain."

Galtero leaned back in his bench, pale. Horror, combined with anger distorted his face. I thought he would either get sick or throw his dagger at me. Ravana bit down on her bottom red lip. The scribe leaned over and whispered something to the false king.

Anger overcame him. "You lie! Do not mock me, girl. You are not describing a hatching. This is your last chance. Tell of a true dragon hatching if you care to live."

He pulled himself to his feet and motioned for the guard to bring my hand to the railing. Galtero leaned forward, his knife at the ready.

I suppressed a shudder at the thought of his knife slicing through my flesh again.

Fighting my panic, and the man who tried to drag me closer to the rail, I asserted, "I do not lie. You asked for a description of a hatching, and that's exactly what you're getting. It is what I, myself, went through. Would you prefer I tone it down so you can feel more at ease?"

He shot me a black look and leveled his blade over the rail.

Black Castle

As I strained against the guards to keep my arm close to my body, and my body away from the rail, my tongue was loosed. Eshshah groaned.

"Because I can dilute it, and make it sound like a cowardly daydream instead of the three-day nightmare that's possible in a hatching. I can neglect to inform you that you could visit your ancestors in the Shadows, where you would beg to stay with them and not return to the pain caused by your dragon. I could omit —"

Galtero jabbed his knife at me. His face, at first white, turned to purple.

I flinched, but thankfully enough distance remained between us, I was beyond his reach.

Abruptly, he halted his attack and shouted, "Away with her. Throw her in the dungeon before I finish her here and now. Insolent, ignorant, stubborn girl. If you weren't my leverage for a dragon egg, I would slash your throat this instant. But, you still have plenty more body parts I can remove if you do not start cooperating. Think about that when you are down there." The veins stuck out in his neck.

I was dragged away, but while he remained within earshot, I yelled over my shoulder, "I tell you the truth." Then lower, so he couldn't hear me, I said, "I hope you choke on it."

The man to my left cuffed me on the back of my head.

Five guards simultaneously pushed and pulled me down a narrow spiral staircase. Eshshah tried to calm me but I was on fire. I struggled to resist them. There was not enough room to fight in the cramped space. I had to halt my struggle, else the result would send us tumbling down the stairs — them crushing me at the bottom.

We reached a damp, dark level. Three of the men held me while another opened a hatch in the dirt floor.

I gazed into the dark hole at my feet. The stench of old bones and death reached me. I realized too late, the penalty for my temper.

One of the guards uncoiled a rope and attempted to tie it around my waist. The thought of spending any time in that black pit gave rise to my panic. I wrestled and kicked as the men tried to get a hold of my chains. Too close to the edge, I lost my balance. My captors grabbed for me, but grasped only air. I plummeted into the dense blackness, screaming in terror.

Exclamations of dismay echoed from the guards.

"Eshshah!" I shrieked as I fell into the pit.

"Amáne," she called in agony.

Is there no bottom?

As that thought completed, my body hit the hard ground, head first. I heard a thump and a squishing sound, like smashing a pumpkin, and felt no more.

Chapter Thirteen

I forced my eyes open. Darkness rushed in around me.

The smell of rot and death. The damp dirt walls. The sweltering heat. The pain in my hand. I'd had this dream before. I bit back a scream.

It's not a dream is it? I am in a dungeon. An oubliette. What crime did I commit to find myself here?

I grabbed my head as an explosion of noise assaulted me. A sound like metal scraping against metal, but in the form of words I couldn't understand.

"Leave me alone," I cried in my madness.

A commotion overhead startled me. Men's voices echoed loudly. A shaft of light entered the blackness.

A torch?

I brought my hands to my face to ward off the painful glare.

"Ho, down there. You alive?"

"If she don't answer this time," another voice said, "yer goin' down there to get 'er. If she's dead, yer the one gonna tell the king, as you bein' the one to let go o' her."

"Yes, I'm alive. Get me out of here," I said in a raspy whisper.

"I didn't let 'er go. You pushed 'er."

"Please help me." I tried louder this time.

"Can ya hear me? Are ya alive down there?"

I took in a painful breath and attempted to shout, "Get. Me. Out!"

"I hear her. She's comin' 'round," said the second voice.

"Well Gahn, be thankful for that," said another. "At least you can keep yer head."

"Yeah, if you hadn't pushed her …"

"I didn't push 'er, she slipped."

The argument above me escalated.

"Stow it. I'll have all yer miserable heads if ya don't do what ya came here fer. Now git her outta there."

"I'm not goin' in that hole if I don't have to," The voice attributed to Gahn echoed above.

A swish of air moved in front of me as something dropped down.

"Grab the rope and tie it around ya," he ordered.

I forced myself to a sitting position, reached out and found the rope. It was thick and rough. After fumbling and trying to work my uncooperative hands, I succeeded in securing it around my waist.

"I'm ready," I called up in a weak voice.

The line tightened and the men pulled me up. Each yank jerked my body. Tears of pain poured down my face.

Free of the oubliette, they steadied me away from the opening. One of the guards undid my chains.

"Ought you to do that?"

"Look at 'er. Does it look like she got any fight in 'er? Don't question me again."

The men surrounded me and led me toward a lit passage.

Delirious, I let them push, pull, drag and carry me up stairs, down corridors and up more stairs until we were above ground in an area that nearly reeked of opulence.

BLACK CASTLE

One of my captors turned to me and said, "Straighten up. Don't dare topple. Yer 'bout to face the king."

They're bringing me before a king?

I sucked in a trembling breath and stood as well as my pain-wracked body would allow.

The large doors opened before us and we stepped into an immense room. Light streamed through the high windows. My eyes went in and out of focus as my head threatened to explode. The king sat atop his throne in the middle of the chamber. A sleek lady in a black cape stood to his right. Her lips red against her pale skin. With her dark dress and the ruby hanging at her forehead, she resembled a black widow spider.

My captors pushed me closer.

"King Galtero, here she is." The guard bowed.

The king uttered a disapproving grunt. His eyes held one of my guards with a dark glare. The man twitched in fear.

"What did you do to her?"

"We didn't do nothin', King Galtero. She fell."

"Couldn't you have cleaned her up?"

"Yes, m'lord, sorry m'lord. We can do that straightaway, m'lord," said the head guard.

The man called Gahn turned to me a with a lewd snicker. "I'll clean 'er up, Yer Magesty."

My stomach clenched.

"Never mind," growled the king. "He'll have to accept her in her present condition."

He addressed an attendant, "Show our guest in."

A door opened to my left and a most striking young noble set foot into the room. Two men accompanied him. The three were similarly dressed in tunics, tights and black knee-high boots. But the younger of the three, the noble, stood out with a regal bearing. The glint of a formidable gold ring on his finger reflected the light from the windows. Behind them followed a dozen nervous-looking armed guards of the same company as those that surrounded me. All with their hands on the hilts of their sheathed swords.

Scrunching my eyes, I tried to focus on the young man's face. The word 'striking' did not do him justice. He was beautiful, if that could be said of a man.

King Galtero cleared his throat. "It appears my staff is not as well trained in hospitality skills as I would have hoped. I will deal with them." He shot a seething look at the man supporting me, who recoiled in reaction to the king's glare.

"I am sure her injuries are minor," he said to his guests.

Why are they discussing me? What would this man care about my injuries?

The striking young man turned to me. I jerked at the shock and anguish in his deep green eyes. They held me as if in a spell. My heart stalled. He started to move in my direction, but was prevented by the king's men nearest him.

Without breaking eye contact, he groaned, "What have they done to you?"

I noted the blood and filth that covered my clothing, the dirty rag that wrapped my finger, and I felt shame for my disheveled appearance in front of this refined lord.

The young noble spun around and lunged in an aggressive move toward the king. I believe he would have slain him that moment if it were possible. His companions got hold of his arms and one of them gave the young man a warning tip of his head.

The sound of dozens of swords being drawn filled the room. My guards crowded around me and brandished their halberds. The king's personal guards raised their crossbows.

Black Castle

"Move against me, Ansel Drekinn, and I'll cut her down, now," King Galtero growled.

Life froze in suspension. Not a movement from any of the room's occupants. A silent battle ensued as Ansel Drekinn and the king pitted glare against blazing glare.

After what seemed an endless space of time, King Galtero barked out a laugh. With a wave of his hand, he said, "Ah, but where are my manners? I gave you safe passage, and I am a man of my word."

His assertion rang of untruth, but the atmosphere in the room lessened its tension.

King Galtero peered at Ansel Drekinn suspiciously and said, "Your arrival in Orchila is certainly sooner than I expected. You must have swift dragons."

The noble locked eyes with the king for an uncomfortable moment before he answered, "Our dragons are swift."

He turned away from the throne and took a few steps closer to me. Two of my guards moved quickly and crossed their halberds to block his advance.

"Amáne? Can you see me? Can you speak? It's Ansel." His suffering seemed as great as mine.

Pain and turmoil spun my thoughts, adding to the confusion of the garbled voice that echoed in my mind.

Amáne? That's one of the words the voice keeps repeating. The only one I can understand.

I dipped down in a painful curtsy. I thought it to be the proper response to the young man. He seemed more royal than the one they called King Galtero.

"I beg your pardon, m'lord — do I know you?"

The man's knees appeared to weaken. I'd caught his agony when I first saw him, but the way his face just paled stole my breath.

"Amáne," he cried.

My heart constricted.

I curtsied again. "Perhaps you have me mistaken for someone else, sir. I am ... that is, my name ... er ... I ..." My mouth went dry.

King Galtero let out a laugh that filled the room. I cringed at the sound.

The pale lady stepped down from the dais and glided close to the young man. She slipped between his companions as she circled him. Tracing her hand along his shoulders and back, she inhaled deeply, appearing to drink in every part of Ansel Drekinn. He stood rigid, unresponsive to her caresses. Stopping before the noble, the black widow ran her fingers over his lips as she observed me out of the corner of her eye. He didn't appear to enjoy her attentions.

I blinked in confusion. *What is she doing?*

She leaned in closer as if to kiss him.

"Enough, Ravana," the king barked. "That is sufficient proof. The girl is oblivious."

Ravana spun on her heels and sulked back up to the side of the throne. Throwing the young man one last hungry look, she turned her attention to King Galtero.

"Ha, Ansel Drekinn, it appears you may be trading your freedom for a half-wit. Deal, or no deal? She is still worth an egg to me. You need but walk away, deliver the egg and you can have what's left of her."

Ansel Drekinn turned to his two companions and gave a small jerk of his head. Both men hesitated, their expressions doubtful.

In an authoritative voice, he said to his men, "Take her out of here. Have Eshshah see to her immediately."

They both dipped their heads and saluted him in a curious fashion. Even in his youth, he outranked the two older men.

He turned to Galtero and said in a strong voice, "You will have me in exchange. But we need two more days to procure the egg."

Galtero's face turned red. After a long silence, he said, "Very well. Two more days. No more!"

The noble's two companions moved toward me. The larger one shoved aside the guards who had crossed their halberds. One of my guards puffed out his chest in defiance, but a withering stare from the man in the black boots was all it took to deflate him. I shrank back at their approach.

"Everything's all right, now, Amáne. We came to help you. Please trust us," said the younger of the two.

"I'm not Amáne, and I don't know who you are."

He blinked in disbelief, but recovered quickly. "I'm Avano. My friend, Braonán and I will take you somewhere safe."

I had nowhere to escape, no strength to fight. The room spun. My vision went dark at the edges. Avano caught me before I crumpled to the ground.

Half conscious, I could feel his long strides as he carried me, hopefully away from this dreadful castle.

We stopped and I could make out the silhouette of Ansel Drekinn bending over me. He softly stroked my hair and kissed my forehead. His scent and his touch were not unpleasant.

I vaguely remembered being carried out of the castle. Bright sunlight warmed my face. I could smell the turf and the aromatic sea air from far off. The difference between that moment and the stifling oubliette in which I'd awoken was like moon and sun.

The name Amáne echoed loudly in my head once again.

"No," I whispered.

"Shh, it's alright. You'll be in a safe place soon," Avano said.

I shook my head from side to side, trying to rid myself of the voice. A pressure on the top of my head sent a relaxing warmth over me. Before I succumbed to this welcomed comfort, I heard Avano say, "The quicker we're out of here, would be to our advantage. Eshshah, Braonán will take her back to the inn. You can continue to treat her once we get there."

In my dream, the sensation of the air moving fast around me almost seemed real.

Chapter Fourteen

Shadows played against my eyelids as I moved into consciousness. I lay on something soft. My eyes were heavy, difficult to open. A weight pressed on my forehead and the scratching voice in my head started again.

"Stop, please. Who are you? Leave me alone," I pleaded. I reached my hand up to remove the weight. Fear gripped me when I touched something solid and smooth. Forcing my eyes open, I found my vision filled with large fangs.

My scream startled the monster that was about to devour me. It pulled its head away as I scrambled backwards like a crab. Pain shot through my body when I fell off the bed. I rose to my feet and moved further from the red dragon until my back pressed against the far wall.

Before I could scream again, the door flew open and two men rushed in, swords drawn. A large man with a beard and a younger good-looking man stood, ready to fight. The two whom I had seen in my nightmare of a castle and a king.

Am I still dreaming?

"Watch out!" I shouted. "Behind you. There's a dragon."

They glanced over their shoulders and then back at me. Both twisted their faces in a puzzled gaze. They sheathed their swords, glanced back at the dragon and then again at me.

"That's Eshshah," the younger man said, in a soothing voice, the way one would speak to a child.

"It's a dragon and it's about to eat me — to eat us all."

"Amáne?" said the younger man.

"I keep telling people I'm not Amáne. I'm ... er ... you can call me Vann. And what do you want with me? Avano, right?"

The castle dream must have been real.

He nodded.

I flattened myself closer to the wall as my eyes went from each man to the dragon. They didn't appear to have any fear of the large creature in the room. In fact, they seemed more concerned with me.

"Don't worry about Eshshah," the young warrior said. He tipped his head, a searching look in his eyes. "She won't hurt you. She's ... that is ... you are ..."

At a gesture from the larger man, he stopped whatever he was about to say, and instead said, "You remembered my name. That's good. In case you've forgotten, this is Braonán. We are at your service." They both bowed.

"Thank you, but I don't need your service. And please don't bow to me. I'm a commoner." I shifted uncomfortably. "Tell your dragon to stop staring at me."

"She's not my — " Avano said. "— Of course. She'll stop staring at you."

As I eyed her a thought crossed my mind. "Is she the noise or voice I've been hearing in my head?" I said.

Avano raised his eyebrows, but gave a slight nod.

"Tell her to stay out of my head."

"As you wish." He turned to Eshshah. Something passed between the two, followed by an apologetic gesture from Avano. For the first time since the oubliette, silence filled me. I breathed a sigh of relief and sneaked a glance at Eshshah. I must have been mistaken — how could a dragon have feelings — but her golden eyes seemed to reflect sorrow.

"Eshshah would like to help you, Amá — Vann. She can heal your injuries." Avano gently explained.

"No! No, please don't let her any closer."

"Avano is right," repeated Braonán. "Eshshah possesses healing powers. She needs more time with you, if you'll only let her —"

"Just keep her away from me. I'm afraid she'll bite me."

"Dragons don't bite," Braonán said.

"Yes, they do. I ... I remember. I was bitten by one once, when I was a small child ... I think. It nearly sent me to my ancestors." My hand went to my temple in a effort to bring back that memory. It slipped away as soon as I had spoken it. It may have just been another one of my dreams.

"I thought there weren't supposed to be any such creatures as dragons," I added.

The two men shot each other a troubling glance before turning their attention back to me.

"Vann, food and a warm bath will do you well," Braonán said. "Avano, I'll send the girl to attend her. As soon as she gets here, you go contact the Healer, then we'll gather the riders for a meeting."

Braonán turned and strode out of the room.

Avano nodded to Eshshah, and again something passed between them, as if she could understand him without him uttering a word. She slid out of the room. I knew nothing of dragons, but I had to admit, she acted forlorn.

Taking in my surroundings, I found myself in a large chamber with an equally large door, like it had been built to allow entry to a dragon. The bed was on the other side of the room. A dip in the floor lay close to the bed.

"What is this place? What am I doing here? Am I your hostage, now?"

"No, you're not a hostage. We're on the island of Orchila, in a building that used to be an inn for us dragon riders."

"Dragon riders?"

My head throbbed. Mentally I'd hit a wall. I swayed. Avano took my arm and gently led me back to the bed. I perched on the edge.

"If I'm not a hostage, then let me leave."

"You're in no condition to go anywhere. Someone is coming to help you get more comfortable. This will all get straightened out. Try not to worry about it."

"Try not to worry about it?" I threw my hands in the air. "I don't remember my past. People are mistaking me for someone named Amáne. I wake up in a room filled with a dragon. You know more than you're telling. And I'm not to worry?" My voice rose with each sentence.

Avano seemed at a loss for words. He opened his mouth to say something, but was saved the trouble as a young girl entered with clothes and towels draped over her arm. She had a dark complexion and long dark hair, a colorful cloth wrapped around her waist for a skirt. Her top, just as colorful, appeared to me that part of it was missing. Her stomach remained bare.

The girl curtsied. "I Mora'ina m' lady —"

"No, don't curtsy to me. Don't call me m' lady."

BLACK CASTLE

"Yes, m' lady. As you wish. Please to come with me."

I looked to Avano. He nodded and backed out the door, leaving me with the native girl.

Mora'ina put a strong arm around my waist, helped me up and led me down a hallway to a human-size door. She opened it and a perfumed steam surrounded me. A bathing room. Finally, something I knew about.

CHAPTER FIFTEEN

I sank down into the hot scented water and searched my shattered mind for what I could remember of dragon lore. It had to be just that — lore, stories, fables. They were mythical creatures. But here, in this place called Orchila, I awoke to one staring me in the face.

I shook my head in disbelief. But however improbable, Eshshah was real. I saw her. I felt her. Braonán and Avano were dragon riders, and they were gathering other riders for a meeting.

The more I searched my memories, the more nothing came to mind. No impression that could help me understand.

How could I be so lost?

A tear slid down my cheek. I took in a shaky breath. Somehow I needed to try to fill in the holes in my damaged memory.

But how?

And what of Eshshah? How could she help me as those two riders say she could?

I realized the pain in my head was nearly gone.

Did the dragon do that? Can she give me back my past? I doubt it.

BLACK CASTLE

The thought of getting that close to her again made me tremble. Seeing her fangs so near terrified me. Still, she didn't deserve the disrespect I'd shown her. I couldn't get over the sorrow in her eyes as she left the room.

Maybe a dragon could get their feelings hurt. I'll have to think of how I can offer her my apology. This is madness — I'm actually talking about seeking pardon from a dragon.

I shook my head. Enough of my debate regarding the emotions of dragons. Truthfully, I needed to concentrate my efforts on bringing back something about my past. Anything. But my recollections went only as far as my release from the oubliette.

My panic rose. Closing my eyes, I took in a large calming breath and released it slowly. After several breaths, my heart slowed its beat.

My concerns wouldn't leave me. What could be the reason for that scene at the castle with the young noble, Ansel Drekinn? His eyes — those green deep eyes that were so full of concern. Now he was in danger on account of me.

Why had such value been placed on my life?

A stranger had exchanged himself as a hostage to give me my freedom. Galtero had said something about trading me for an egg. What kind of egg would be worth human lives?

What have I gotten into? Who am I?

Ansel Drekinn acted as if he knew me, somehow. Perhaps I was a member of his staff. Maybe part of the kitchen help, or a handmaiden to his lady.

Does he have a lady?

Someone of that station and those looks, I was sure, had a lady, or more likely many ladies vying for his attention. A twinge of envy shot through me. I nearly laughed out loud. It was preposterous that a commoner, like me, should dare entertain even one thought of being anything other than staff. I probably was not even that. But, the probability he knew me wouldn't go away.

Sighing, I slipped down lower in the tub and proceeded to wash the stench that lingered on my skin from the oubliette and whatever else happened in that castle. I gasped. What I'd thought to be dirt and dried blood on my right shoulder turned out to be a tattoo-like mark. It was the likeness of a dragon. It didn't come off, as hard as I scrubbed. My skin went raw from the effort.

I nearly inhaled the bath water as I discovered another tattoo on my ankle. It, too was in the likeness of a dragon, but misshapen and evil looking.

Why do I have a dragon on my shoulder and another on my ankle?

I must have known more about dragons than I'd thought. Perhaps I'd been a stable hand for dragons.

Do dragons live in stables?

Too many unanswered questions. My head started to throb again. The room began to spin. Mora'ina entered the bath chambers before the pressure that weighed on my chest could send me into hysterics.

I didn't like being waited on, but truthfully, I couldn't have managed to exit the tub without her assistance. Mora'ina wrapped me in a thick robe and guided me back to my room. She helped me into a chair at a chamber table where a tray of small cakes dipped in honey and a serving of tea had been placed. A small vial of a dark liquid sat beside the tray.

"Small eat, now. Big meal in dining hall. Take." She picked up the tray and offered me its contents. I chose a cake and pushed it in my mouth. Mora'ina nodded in approval. The cake was sweet and light. Closing my eyes, I enjoyed the delicate flavor. I followed it with the tea she poured. It was a bit annoying having her hover over me, nodding at every bite I took, but I did my best to ignore her.

After I'd devoured several cakes, Mora'ina picked up the vial, uncorked it and put it in my hand. "Vann must drink. Make Vann strong. Dragon men wait long time for talk."

"They're waiting for me?"

Mora'ina nodded. "Take now." She nudged my hand that held the vial. "Take tea after."

I hesitated, alternately eyeing the vial and then her. I brought it close and took a sniff. My eyes squeezed shut, my nose wrinkled. I glanced up at the native girl, who dipped her head expectantly.

As if she read my mind, she said, "Not poison. Drink."

Closing my eyes again, I held my breath and tipped the contents back. It was like swallowing fire. The draught burned a path down my throat. I broke into a coughing fit. My eyes teared as I fought to breathe. Just as quickly, the discomfort left. I felt a surge of strength fill me. My fatigue dissolved, my mind cleared. Hope soared momentarily, but the dark liquid did not bring back my lost past.

I wiped the back of my hand across my mouth and turned to Mora'ina. "What was that?" My voice came out in a hoarse whisper.

"Magic herb from Great Healer of far kingdom, Tera-vin-eiya."

"It was more like liquid fire," I said. But truthfully, it had done wonders.

She nodded and said. "Now Vann fast put dress." She held up a beautiful blue gown.

"What is this?" I said. "I don't dress in such extravagance."

Mora'ina wouldn't hear my protests. Without another word, she had me wrapped in the silky fabric.

They must not have anything else for me to wear.

I found the gown quite uncomfortable. Not only because it was so confining, but more that I felt out of place wearing it. I ran my hand along the fabric. These are not the skirts of a commoner.

I moved away from Mora'ina's fussing over my dress. "Thank you, Mora'ina. Whose clothes are these anyway? They seem to be made for someone my size."

The girl nodded as she buckled a narrow belt around my waist then handed me a pair of slippers.

She rushed me to the other end of the inn and we entered the dining hall. Long tables with benches on either side took up the room, occupied mostly by men and a few women in uniform — obviously soldiers. Others were dressed similar to Braonán and Avano — dragon riders.

Heads turned at my entrance. I froze as I took in the noisy hall. One or two rose from their seats and began to bow. They caught themselves straight off and sat quickly.

It must be a common reaction to bow whenever a female enters a room. Why did they then decide not to?

Shaking my head, I tried to back out of the room. Mora'ina had a firm hold on me. Avano stepped forward, "Vann, it's all right. These are all your friends." He turned to face the group and said, "Dragon riders, soldiers, meet Vann." He put extra emphasis on my name.

They all smiled or nodded and pronounced various greetings. The room buzzed with their well-wishes.

I blew out a few short breaths, swallowed and worked at placing an appreciative smile on my face. Words wouldn't form, so I curtsied.

For a fleeting instant, I caught a look of shock on a couple of the riders.

Black Castle

"Vann," said Braonán, "let me show you the proper response to dragon riders. No need to curtsy. Place your hand like this." He put his thumb and forefinger together to form an "o." The other three fingers remained straight, as he put his hand to his heart and saluted.

"This is the dragon salute. It is all that is needed. It's also how to greet and show respect for our dragons."

Still standing stiffly at the doorway, I saluted the riders as I'd been shown. A couple riders flinched and seemed like they were about to return the salute.

Avano led me to an available bench. "Please join us. I'm sure you're as hungry as we are."

I stepped over the bench, trying to take my seat in a lady-like manner, cursing the gown as I adjusted it around me. Avano slid in to my right.

It dawned on me I hadn't any idea of how long it had been since I'd eaten, besides the few bites of the cakes Mora'ina had brought. The aroma of the foods wafted toward me.

There was something about the comfort of food and the appeasement of hunger that put me in an amiable mood. I found myself laughing with the riders at my table, like I'd known them all along.

Chapter Sixteen

Slowly the room thinned out as the group finished their meals and excused themselves. Only a handful of us remained in the dining hall.

I moved my knife in circles around the gravy left on my plate, brooding about my next move.

Where am I to go? How do I remedy my situation? What of Ansel Drekinn?

A rider entered the room.

"Braonán, Avano," he said, "the Healer is back on the communication disc. She is anxious to speak with ... uh, Vann." He shot me a concerned glance.

"Thank you, Eben, we'll be right in," Braonán said.

Braonán turned to me, "Vann, let me explain what you're about to see. Dragon riders have a way of communicating from a distance. That is, besides riding our dragons that distance and meeting in person. We use a device called the communication disc. You may not know that our dragons have names, and the meaning of their names manifests in their scales. In other words, Eshshah, for instance, means fire. You'll find that if you hold one of her scales and whisper, 'Eshshah,' the scale will create a flame."

He smiled at my incredulity, but continued his instruction. "One of us riders, Gallen, had a dragon named Gyan. His name meant knowledge. Gallen created this device with his dragon's scales. Speaking the name, Gyan, and then the name of the rider we wish to contact, allows us to communicate with that rider just as effectively as if in person.

"The Healer, who holds a high position in our court as healer and advisor to the king, has asked to speak with you. She would like to assess your ... condition."

I wondered if she was the Great Healer Mora'ina mentioned. My stomach quaked.

Braonán continued, "Don't be alarmed when you see the communication disc. The only way I can describe it, is it's like seeing your reflection in a mirror, but it will not be your face staring out. In this case, it will be the Healer, who is located far away."

I nodded.

Avano and Braonán ushered me through a door to an anteroom off of the dining hall. A man was speaking. I caught a part of his conversation. "Sovann informed us Lord Ansel is adamant we make every effort to save her."

A female voice responded, "We can only hope she's not already lost ..."

She cut her statement short when I entered.

Avano took my arm and led me to the far corner of the room. A device hung on the wall. A thick glass disc, about two hands-width in diameter, was mounted on a wooden background. Behind the glass, an inlay of three dragon scales were set in a triangular formation. Below the glass disc, a brass knob protruded.

"Thank you, Calder," Avano said. "If you'll move to the right and keep hold of the knob, I'll let Vann stand here in front."

The device was mounted at a level more suitable to the men's height, but if I stretched to my fullest, I could peer into it. The glass reflected a rather striking lady, possibly in her fifties. I noted her kind expression, but also recognized she was someone with whom one would not want to displease. Her eyes bore into mine.

I gasped. It was a bit unsettling gazing into what seemed like a looking glass and not seeing my own face. Although, at the moment even my own face was hardly familiar.

My throat tightened at the concern that registered in her eyes. A man stepped into view beside her. A nice-looking man, about the same age, with long blonde hair.

"Healer and Gallen," Avano said, "let me introduce Vann." Again, he held my name for longer than I felt necessary.

I curtsied. "Lady Healer, Sir Gallen."

Avano cleared his throat. "They're both dragon riders," he said out of the corner of his mouth.

"Oh!" I said. I saluted them in the manner I'd recently learned. Their smiles warmed my heart.

"Pleased to meet you, Vann. I hope that you're feeling better. Do you mind if I ask you a few questions?"

"No, m'lady."

Her eyebrows drew together, slightly.

"Vann," the Healer said, "do you remember how you came to be at the inn?"

"Yes, m'lady. That is, some of it. A noble named Ansel Drekinn came to the castle where I'd been a prisoner. I believe he may have been searching for someone. Instead he found me. The lord stayed in exchange for my freedom. I don't know why. Do you know of him?"

"What do you recall of your time at the castle?"

Black Castle

"Only that I awoke in an oubliette and the guards hoisted me out and took me to the king."

"King?"

"Yes. King Galtero." I swiped a strand of hair from my face.

The Healer's eyes opened wide as her attention was drawn to my hand. "Do you know what happened to your finger?"

"No, m'lady."

I gripped my deformed hand and held it to my chest.

"May I ask you a question, Lady Healer?"

"Yes, of course."

"Can you heal me? Can you give me back my past?" I didn't mean for my voice to tremble.

A shadow crossed her face. "I'm afraid, Vann, you're suffering from a condition call amnesia, a loss of memory. Yours is a rare case, indeed. It's not common to lose one's entire identity. And to complicate matters, you are ... that is, you have an additional ... connection ... a link ..." She halted her discourse. "I'm sorry, but it could be damaging to rush, or try and force your memories. Your recollections must come in a natural sequence, internally, from your own state of awareness. You have to take it slowly." She let out a sigh. "Fortunately, the majority of amnesia cases resolve themselves within a few days. Let's hope you find yourself in that company."

"Is it possible I may never recover my memory?"

"Like I said, we will hope you make a full recovery." Her expression became more serious. "I'm told you won't allow Eshshah close to you," she said.

I pressed my lips together.

The Healer nodded slowly.

CHAPTER SEVENTEEN

While Braonán stayed and spoke with the Healer, Avano escorted me out of the anteroom. He gestured to me to take a seat at the table where we had recently eaten.

"Who is the lady you need to save?" I asked.

He gave me a questioning look.

"I heard them talking about saving someone, and the Healer said she hoped she was not already lost. Do you have a plan to find this lady? Is she on the island? And what about Lord Ansel Drekinn? Do you have the egg of which the king spoke? Is it a dragon egg? That's what's needed to win him his freedom, correct?"

"Whoa. Too many questions. I can tell you this much, we had formed a plan to find 'this lady.' But, when Eshshah announced ..." Avano stopped and appeared to choose his next words carefully, "...announced a ... a misfortune had befallen her rider — the lady — plans ... er ... changed. We were forced to go forward with an alternate strategy. It was not one in which we riders agreed. The king could not be dissuaded. He insisted he would go directly to Galtero and negotiate."

BLACK CASTLE

"King? Who? You're telling me Ansel Drekinn is a king also? What ...? Why...?" I swung my leg over the bench and jumped up. Pacing the floor, I raked my fingers through my hair.

"How is it I, a commoner, am involved with a royal, no two royals? Why would King Ansel exchange himself for me?"

"First of all, King Ansel is not a king, *also*. He is *the* king. Galtero is not a king at all. Secondly, common born or not, you were a captive of Galtero. King Ansel negotiated for your freedom. Vann, I'm afraid too much information may not do you well. I've told you enough. Perhaps too much. You heard the Healer. For now, we need to take caution on what we reveal."

He rose and stood before me, preventing further pacing. "There is something I need to discuss with you."

"What?" My shoulders tightened.

"It would be to our advantage if you could help us."

I looked behind me over my right shoulder, then my left in a dramatic show. Placing my hand on my chest, I locked eyes with Avano. "You're asking for my help? With what, exactly? I have no skills that I know of. You do understand I have no past? I gaze in the looking glass and a stranger stares back at me. How could I ever be of any help?"

"Can you fight?"

"Fight? You mean use a sword?"

"Or a spear, a glaive, any kind of martial arts? Would you be willing to ride a dragon?"

"Ride a dragon?" I nearly choked. "No! To all of the afore mentioned. Why would you ask such questions?"

"I'm asking because I want to see how you answer, Vann. How do you know you can't fight? That you don't have the courage to get in a saddle? Have you given up? You've already resigned yourself to the fact you can't help?"

"That's not it. I just ... I ... Do you have any idea what it's like for me? What I'm going through?" My voice quavered.

"Move on, Vann. Don't sit back and do nothing because you're feeling sorry for yourself!"

Anger sparked hot in my blood. I opened my mouth to spew every kind of insult at him.

Avano held his hands up in surrender, then said, "I'm sorry. I've overstepped my bounds." His eyes fell for a breath before he brought them up to meet mine. "Truthfully, I think you are capable of more than you know."

My shoulders dropped. I heaved a loud sigh of frustration and shook my head. Thankful I hadn't said what I felt like saying, I allowed my heart to slow its beat.

Maybe he's right. Maybe I have given up.

Closing my eyes, I tipped my head back. A tear escaped.

In a quieter voice, I said, "I wake up in a hole, half mad, with screeching voices exploding in my head, my finger severed," I raised my left hand in front of his face, "my memories gone. Some man I don't even know traded his freedom for mine. A king, no less. And now I find you think I'm capable of taking up a weapon, or sitting atop a dragon." I threw my hands up.

Avano let out a long breath. "Yes, that about sums it up."

Some man? Did I just call King Ansel Drekinn 'some man'?

I slumped down to the bench and put my head in my hands. "I need to know who I am."

"I'm sorry, Vann. That, I can't give you. We can't force your memories."

I sat in silence for several moments, feeling Avano's eyes on me. Lifting my face, I straightened up and said, "Fine. I'm not without my own sense of duty. I owe it to King Ansel Drekinn. Get me a weapon, I'll do what I can — short of riding a dragon. I'd planned on helping you anyway."

Avano jerked his head back. After a pause, he broke into laughter. "Of course you did," he said, "of course. I expected as much."

He summoned Mora'ina and instructed her to find me some suitable clothes for sword practice.

Turning to me, Avano said, "Meet me on the practice field."

Chapter Eighteen

Avano handed me a spear. A straight two-sided blade on the end of a pole, half-an-arm's length taller than I. A crossguard jutted out below the base of the blade. I hefted it, then executed a couple of practice thrusts and cuts. My actions surprised me.

How would I have known the moves I just made?

Avano raised an eyebrow. "I wanted to let you get the feel of this glaive. I'm pleased to see you're comfortable enough with it."

He took back the glaive and placed it on a nearby wagon that held a number of other weapons.

"We'll be practicing with these wooden spears. They have round blunts on the end. We'll also use wooden wasters instead of real swords. I need to see what you can do with a spear as well as a sword."

He turned back to the wagon. "I've also brought some armor that may fit you. It's not your standard armor. Under the leather exterior, these pieces are crafted from dragon scales. The toughest material available."

I admired the worked leather. He detached a corner of the front piece and lifted it. I gasped at the dragon scales underneath. They shimmered ember red, the same color as Eshshah.

"I'll help you," he said. "Let's start with your leg pieces. The greaves for your shins, poleyn above the greaves, cuisses go on your thighs."

He helped me don my breastplate, then picked up the pieces for my shoulders.

"Those are pauldrons, aren't they?"

I knew the name. I smiled.

"Very good," Avano said.

The other pieces didn't come to mind as he named and secured rarebrace on my upper arms; couter for my elbows, the vambrace below that.

The helmet was like a leather skull cap, but also constructed with dragon scales between two supple layers of leather. Straps buckled under my chin. Avano showed me a small lever near my temple, that when pushed down, a pair of protective lenses lowered over my eyes.

"These are dragon scales, treated and polished to perfect clarity," he said.

I pulled on the most comfortable gloves, which Avano assured me were more protective than any gauntlets found in regular armor.

Taking up a waster for each of us, he handed me one.

"Ready?" he said. He pointed his sword at me.

I gave him a doubtful nod. A nervous sweat broke out on my face.

Avano didn't wait another breath before he lunged at me and executed a series of strikes. I parried all of them. Just as I felt a sense of accomplishment, he changed his timing and whacked my shoulder. I yelped, then tipped my head as I conceded that round to him.

We began again. Avano made it a point to exploit my every mistake. Eventually, I adapted to his style and reacted quickly to each of his moves. He gave me pointers and added praise when I succeeded in a hit.

Trading the wasters for the practice spears, we continued sparring.

I was pleased with my newly-discovered talent. But, it only made me more desperate to find out who I was, and why I would know how to wield weapons at this skill level.

I chanced an attempt at conversation. "So if you can't give me any information about who I am, the least you could do is tell me about yourself, Avano."

"Not much to tell," he said, not missing a step in his advance. "Been a dragon rider since before you were born."

He brought his spear in a downward motion.

I leapt aside and redirected his swing.

"I was a foot soldier before that. I've seen and done more than a man's lifetime should hold."

Breathing heavy, I continued my queries. "Any family?" I tried to bring my weapon behind his leg to trip him.

He anticipated my move and sidestepped. "No. Never had time for any of that."

"At the risk of being too forward, I'd say you need someone, Avano. You should find a lady."

He blinked, but didn't break his concentration.

We circled each other, trying to detect an opening or weakness.

"I like you, Avano. I like you a lot." I said between breaths.

He jabbed. I evaded.

I lunged at him. He parried.

His eyes darted to mine. A strange light in them gave me pause.

"As a brother, I mean!" A blush rose in my face. I lowered my guard.

Avano swung toward my head. He couldn't check his swing. I ducked as his spear arced over me.

Ignoring his near miss, I put up my hand, palm out. Cutting off his imminent reprimand, I said, "Wait! Are you and I ... am I your ... I mean are we ..."

"No, no, no, no! We are not a we!"

"You don't have to be so emphatic about it." I stomped my foot.

"I'm sorry, I didn't mean to sound so harsh. I've loved you since we first met, but as a sister. That's all. No, you and I are not anything but friends. Truthfully."

"Do I have ... someone?"

"Practice is over, Vann. You did well." He spun around to leave the field.

I ran up behind him and grabbed his arm to make him turn to me.

"That's not fair. I need to know. What was my life like? You knew me before ... before this." I swept my hand up to my head. "Why won't you help me? I just need to know if I had someone."

"Amá — Vann, not now."

"You started to call me Amáne again. I'm not Vann, am I? My name *is* Amáne, isn't it?"

I squeezed his arm and drew his eyes to mine.

He sighed. "Yes. That's your name. Please don't ask me anything else."

I could see his distress but I wanted to push him further. I inhaled to press on. Letting my breath out, I dropped my eyes and acquiesced with a nod. My teeth clenched, my eyes burned.

"Go get cleaned up, Amáne," Avano said. "Meet us back in the dining hall in two hours."

He turned and strode away.

Chapter Nineteen

A whirlwind swirled through my thoughts. Instead of heading in to the bathing room, I found myself moving toward a far field. In the fading light, I could see Eshshah in the distance. A huge golden dragon lay next to her. I wondered if it was her mate. They both picked up their heads and watched my approach. My steps slowed.

The large gold, touched his nose to the smaller red. He turned and leaped into the air. I stopped and watched his graceful, yet frightening ascent. His wingspan was imposing.

Wanting to pivot and run for shelter, I fought the urge and held my breath. I summoned my courage and continued to move toward Eshshah. Coming as close as I dared, I lowered myself to the ground, sat cross-legged and faced her. If she wanted to flame me, she could probably still reach. She didn't move, but only watched me with her golden eyes. An intelligence I didn't expect reflected brightly.

"Er ... majestic Eshshah," I said as I gave her the dragon salute. She tipped her head. Her eyes seemed to light up even more.

Fear overcame me. Instead of finishing my greeting, I scooted back further. "With all due respect, don't be offended, but I remind you, please do not get into my head."

Her eyes dulled slightly.

"I came here because I just ... uh ... felt I owe you an apology for my rudeness earlier. I don't know if you can understand me, but I ... I'm sorry for being unkind to you. I don't know anything about dragons, or if you even know what I'm saying, but ..." I shrugged.

The red dragon surprised me with a movement of her head.

"Did you just nod at me?"

She bobbed her head again.

"You understand what I'm saying?"

Again, an affirmative motion.

I let out a long breath. Dropping my eyes, I picked up a handful of sand and let it sift through my fingers. My lips pressed together as I searched my memories. Maybe something I knew about dragons would surface. Nothing.

I couldn't stop my eyes from welling up. The air around me hummed. Blinking back my tears of frustration, I raised my head and noted the humming came from Eshshah. She droned a relaxing tune that emanated from her chest, or possibly her long elegant neck.

I smiled. "You ... give me comfort, Eshshah. Thank you."

Rising to my feet, I saluted her again and backed away. "I have to go now, but if it's alright with you, maybe I can come back. I could use someone to talk to." I laughed to myself at what I'd just said. Somehow it didn't seem as unbelievable as I would have thought only a short while ago. I spun around and ran back toward the inn.

I exited my chambers and met up with Avano as he came down the corridor. Giving him the dragon salute, I fell into step beside him. We made our way to the dining hall.

Several eyes turned in our direction as we entered. I saluted the riders and nodded at the soldiers who had gathered in the hall. To those that greeted me using the name Vann, I told them in a stuttering voice my real name was Amáne.

They smiled or tipped their heads, but otherwise didn't make an issue of this revelation.

The kitchen staff scurried around the tables, mouth-watering aromas rose from the plates they carried. Silence filled the room as we all set ourselves to eating. Once the last dish was cleared and the pitchers of ale were nearly empty, Braonán stood to address the group.

"Riders and soldiers, we're down to our last details for our mission. All the pieces have come together and our operation begins tomorrow at dawn."

"Tomorrow?" I blurted out loud. All eyes turned to me. I slapped my hand over my mouth and fought the red rising in my face.

"I beg your pardon. I'm sorry," I said. "I thought maybe we had more time."

"I'm afraid we've run out. If we don't get our king out by tomorrow evening ..."

I dipped my head.

Braonán went on, "Sovann is keeping us abreast of King Ansel's location in the castle."

I leaned in to Avano and said, "Who's Sovann?"

"King Ansel's dragon."

"The beautiful golden one?"

He nodded.

"How does he know where King Ansel is and how does he keep Braonán informed?"

Avano held up his hand. "I'll fill you in later."

"They are moving his location every few hours," Braonán said. "Galtero is taking no chances. King Ansel is, at present, being kept relatively comfortable. I'm sure Galtero's hospitality will not last much longer. He will, no doubt, have a double-cross in his plans. Even if we were to comply with his demands for an egg, I am certain we wouldn't get our king back alive.

"The components for the explosives have arrived from Serislan. The blast sticks have been assembled."

I turned to Avano, shrugged my shoulders and mouthed "Serislan? Blast sticks?" Again, he gestured for my patience.

I sighed and attempted, with my limited knowledge, to absorb as much information from Braonán as I could.

Braonán's eyes scanned the group and rested on me. He must have sensed my frustration. "To bring you to date, Amáne, we've been searching for Galtero since his escape when we defeated him in the War of the Crown. Our victory put King Ansel, the rightful heir, on the throne of Teravinea. By instigating this ... situation ... Galtero has given away his location. Once we've extracted our king, this is our chance to capture or eliminate this man, for good. We cannot let him escape this time."

He paused to let the significance of his statement sink in, then continued, "Serislan is our ally to the north of Teravinea. King Tynan of Serislan has a team that is known for its knowledge of explosives. They were instrumental in our success to win back the crown from Galtero. Serislan has supplied us with the materials we needed for this mission. Normally, these devices are made with a heavy parchment outer cover, but bamboo is more readily available here, so we improvised.

"We have been in contact with Lia'ina, inside the castle. She is the tribal chief's daughter, the same tribe as Mora'ina. Lia'ina is also a captive, but is allowed moderate freedom. She is head of the kitchen staff. An acquaintance of hers, here in the village, delivers foods and goods daily to Galtero. She has put us in contact with this supplier. He agreed to help us infiltrate the castle.

"We will conceal the explosives in bags of grain. Rider Perrin, being the smallest among us, will be stowed away in a crate to be a part of the morning's delivery. Once inside the castle, he will set the explosives."

I glanced over to the rider of whom Braonán spoke. A serious man, thin perhaps, but small? Not one of these dragon riders would be what I considered small.

A ripple went through my stomach. I had to swallow to keep my dinner down. My mouth moved, but nothing came out. I cleared my throat and managed to whisper, "Excuse me, Braonán." I rose to my feet.

He gave me a questioning stare.

I took in a breath. "I'm sorry to interrupt you again, but I couldn't help but notice I'm much smaller than Perrin."

A low murmur, mostly snickers, swept the room. My eyes flashed. "I'm serious. A crate sized to fit Perrin might bring attention. It would take a much smaller and less conspicuous box to conceal me than it would him. Having said that, I ask that you choose me for that assignment instead of Perrin."

Did I just volunteer to go back into the black castle?

My knees went weak, but I stayed on my feet and forced a resolute expression on my face. Avano snapped his head in my direction. I felt the eyes of all in the room, but I would not be swayed.

Braonán rubbed his beard and frowned. He stood in thought for what felt like forever. Finally, he spoke slowly and deliberately, "You have a good point, and a viable solution. However, with your recent injuries and ... uh ... current ... condition, I'm reluctant to allow you this role. I'd planned on using you as a back up, in a surveillance position. Possibly on Eshshah."

Black Castle

My response was instant, and loud. "I recall enough of my past to know King Ansel is in this circumstance because of me. My sense of duty for his sacrifice demands I do what I can to extricate him, and not stand back and watch in safety. I ask that you strongly consider my offer. In my opinion it's an improvement over your original plan."

Avano cleared his throat loudly. The room fell silent. Sweat beaded across my nose.

Maybe I overstepped my bounds.

Braonán scowled.

I opened my mouth to apologize, but before I could say anything, Braonán simply said, "I don't see this as a plan to which King Ansel would readily agree."

"King Ansel doesn't need to know. Not until I'm safely in."

I caught a glint in Braonán's eye. His mouth lifted as if he remembered a private joke. He struggled for a moment and then, exhaling, turned to Perrin. "We will put you in the air, Perrin, Amáne will take your place in a smaller crate."

Encouraging comments echoed throughout the room.

To me he said, "We'll take your measurements and construct a new crate. You will be instructed on the use of the explosives when this meeting adjourns."

I nodded, and quickly took my seat before my knees gave out.

Feeling Avano's stare, I swung my head toward him. "What?"

He smiled. "You did well. Just what I would have expected from you, Amáne."

"So there's hope for me, yet?"

"There's always hope."

"And hope better not disappoint" I said under my breath.

CHAPTER TWENTY

The riders and soldiers filed out of the dining hall leaving me with Braonán and Avano. Calder came back in with a roll of sail cloth. Carefully unfolding his package, he unveiled a small collection of bamboo segments — both ends sealed, with a cord fixed at one end.

"What are they?" I said.

Braonán chose one and holding it up, said, "This is a blast stick. It is filled with black blasting powder, a chemical explosive. Sulfur and charcoal act as fuels, and sodium nitrate is the oxidizer. When ignited, it will create enough of an explosion to burst through rock."

He handed the stick to me. I held it with respect.

How fascinating that a piece of bamboo the length of my forearm could house a material with such power.

"So, I'm to place these in strategic areas in the castle?"

"Not in the castle, but at the outside walls. We want to create diversions and get Galtero's men mustering their defense as if from an outside assault. Placing the blast sticks in tactical areas can direct his soldiers away from where they are holding King Ansel. I am certain they will not all make off and leave him on his own, but if we can lessen the numbers guarding him, King Ansel can deal with those left."

I nodded slowly.

Braonán unrolled a map and spread it on the table. It depicted the layout of the black castle.

"This floorplan has been given to us by an old villager. He told us his tribe's ancestors were forced to build the castle a couple generations ago. The plans have been handed down through the years. We are fortunate they have allowed us possession. This map shows us not only the configuration of the outside walls, but also the interior chambers and the secret corridors they constructed."

He smoothed the edges of the rolled parchment and placed some tankards on the corners to keep it from rolling back up.

Braonán leaned over the table and paused over the detailed drawing. "I believe we can get the results we need with only two walls targeted." He indicated the western and the southern walls.

"What of the north wall?" I asked.

"That entire area is still in ruins. Galtero is restoring the castle. The north section has very little, if any, reconstruction." He waved his hand over that section.

"According to natives of this island, in the time of their grandfathers a man by the name of Berdosa enslaved their tribe. Under the watch of his henchmen and the loss of many of the tribe's ancestors, the fortress was erected. They were forced to work all hours of the day and night, and construction was completed in record time. Even at that, it took years. The tyrant ignored all advice against building it in such close vicinity of the mountain. He could not be dissuaded from his grandiose plan of completing his legacy. Berdosa assumed since he built on higher ground, he would be safe if the volcano blew. He was wrong. He didn't yet know its fury. The eruption was so great, much of the lava overflowed in the direction of the castle, as did the ash and fumes. That section was destroyed. No one survived."

"What is it about evil people," I said, "that they believe they're superior to everyone else, and disdain any who might know better than they?"

Braonán shook his head.

"How do you know, or, how does Sovann know where King Ansel is?"

Avano took on my question. "Dragons and their riders communicate by thought transference. They can essentially speak with each other without words even when apart. The distance at which they can converse varies with each pair. King Ansel and Sovann have a long thought-transference range. They're in almost constant contact."

"Speak without words? That sounds ..." Before I finished my sentence, a vague memory flashed. My hand shot to my temple, but the thought was gone before I could get a hold of it. I grunted.

"What is it?" Avano asked.

"I ... just ... it's nothing. I'm fine."

He gave me a sidelong glance.

"Where exactly do I have to plant these blast sticks?" I said quickly.

After a moment's pause, Braonán answered, "We've calculated they would best be used at this point on the west wall, here, and in two spots here on the south wall." He put his finger on each spot.

"When the fortress was built, drain spouts were put low in these walls. Their positions line up, near enough, under the harpoon cannons."

BLACK CASTLE

"Harpoon cannons?"

"Anti-dragon artillery. A harpoon shot at the right spot, can bring a dragon down."

My eyes widened. The thought of losing one of those majestic, yet frightening beings was incomprehensible.

"Let us go over our strategy," said Braonán. "The goods are brought in near an entrance in the western wall. Here." He indicated the location on the map.

"They are unloaded from the cart and left in a small courtyard just outside of the kitchen. Lia'ina and her kitchen workers take the supplies from there and haul them in to the storerooms."

"Does anyone ever search the supply cart, or any of the deliveries?" I asked.

"Yes. But there is a space of a few days between inspections, we're told. They just searched a day prior. We are assured we will have a clear pass for the next day or three," he said.

I exhaled a sigh of relief.

"Once inside, Lia'ina will help you out of the crate. She'll give you a hiding place where you are to remain until nightfall."

I nodded.

"From the kitchen, it is an easy trek to the west wall. You will have to move with caution. The guards' locations are not where I would position them, considering the circumstances. But his is to our advantage. None-the-less, they are present in adequate numbers.

"When you deem it safe, you will cross the yard and wedge the first blast stick in the drain spout, here." He showed me a point on the map. "Be sure it is a spout that is under a harpoon cannon. This will ensure that not only will that section of the wall come down, but also their greatest weapon against our dragons. You shouldn't have a problem finding the correct locations."

He moved his hand along the parchment as he briefed me on the areas I would need to access in order to place the other two blast sticks. I was pleased to hear there was a passage inside the west exterior wall. It would get me from where I'd placed the first explosive to the next location.

"To access the passage," Braonán instructed, "look for a push-rock about your shoulder height."

"A push-rock?"

"An opening mechanism. It is approximately the size of my hand." He opened his hand and held it flat. "A rock that looks just a bit different than the rest of the wall, barely perceptible. Push on it and the hidden door will slide open."

Braonán continued his instructions, telling me once the three blast sticks were set, my next step would be to ignite the fuses. I would be shooting an arrow with one of the red dragon's scales secured at the tip. He said whispering Eshshah's name as I released the shaft would cause the scale to emit a small flame as it approached its destination.

Calder, who'd been quiet up to this point, spoke up. "It'll be up to you to decide from which positions you'll ignite the blast sticks. I recommend the first two shots be taken from somewhere near this fountain. It's within range of two of the drain spouts. You'll have to move to set up your last shot."

Am I really going through with this? A ripple of fear shot through me. I shook off the negative thought.

I will succeed.

"Once the explosions are set off," continued Braonán, "you will proceed to the escape tunnel in the old north kitchen, in the ruined section. It is some distance from the third blast stick. Stay close to the castle. Go back toward the fountain and come around this corner. There should be enough distraction by this time. No one should detect you."

Braonán traced the map from the south wall, to the fountain, then to a chamber in the north section. "This is the old kitchen. The area is still in disrepair. The chance of encountering anyone will be minimal. You will find the trap door in the floor about here. Close it after you and latch it from the inside.

"The tunnel is long, but it's another hidden passage we believe they don't know about. You should have no trouble navigating it."

I suppressed a shudder at the thought of the enclosed tunnel.

"There is an exit passage about midway, here." His finger stopped along the diagram of the tunnel. It opens somewhere in the middle of the jungle. You will not use this exit, but continue to the end at the north shore. I'll be waiting for you there," Braonán said.

"What about King Ansel? I thought I was to help him escape."

"The explosions and the chaos it will create is all the help he'll need. As soon as your first blast goes off, all the riders will take to the air, their dragons flaming and the riders loosing arrows. We will also have a small company of bowmen on the ground, posted in various locations around the castle.

"You are to make your escape once the sticks have been set off. King Ansel is confident he can dispatch the guards left around him and meet Avano over here at the west wall."

Avano reached to his side and unlatched a dragon scale that had been carved into the shape of a key. It had a flat brass head on the end, decorated with swirling etchings, including the word, 'Aperio.'

He handed it to me and said, "This is Aperio's key. It will open any lock that may bar your way. Say the name of the late dragon, Aperio, and it will open for you. King Ansel has a key as well."

I turned the key over in my hand, admiring the engravings and shaking my head at the unbelievable attributes of dragon scales.

"The clothing you'll be wearing on this mission," Avano said, "will have a small pocket sewn in your sleeve at the wrist. You can store the key in there."

I nodded as I tightened my hand around the key.

"I have another item for you." He slipped his hand under his sleeve and brought out a black dragon scale. "This is a scale from a living dragon-like creature. His name is Charna Yash-churka. We call him Charna for short."

"A dragon-like creature?" *More mythical beings?*

Avano dipped his head. "We've recently discovered that his scales, like those of our full dragons, exhibit special properties."

I stretched out my hand for the onyx scale. He pulled it from my reach.

"This scale has very serious attributes — much more than most of the others. Charna Yash-churka means black lizard. His scale, when you hold it in front of you and direct its power toward your enemy, will plummet that person into a nightmare of darkness and blindness. If you need to use it, take caution to consciously direct the action toward your intended goal. It could affect anyone in the vicinity, including yourself, if you aren't clear on your target. Trust me, it's a horrifying experience. The effects last quite a long time, unless a dragon pulls you out sooner."

"You've undergone this darkness?"

"Yes. All of us riders tested Charna's scales not many days ago." He gave a quick shake of his head as if to rid himself of the memory.

I grimaced at the scale as he handed it to me.

Black Castle

"No need to fear it, just be heedful."

I took it from his hand and held it with Aperio's key.

"Do you have any questions or are there any points we have covered that you would like to discuss?" Braonán asked.

"Er ... that is ... what if ..." My voice came out in a hoarse whisper. *I can't believe what I'm about to propose.*

I exhaled.

"Yes?" he said.

Braonán's, Avano's and Calder's eyes were all on me.

I sucked in a breath. "It seems that thought transference ... thing ... you all have with your dragons is very useful. With King Ansel in one part of the castle, you riders in the air, and me, by myself ... somewhere else, well ... it would only make sense that I should be a part of that communication."

Avano raised his eyebrows and nodded for me to continue. I wished one of them would have caught on and finished my thought for me. I had a feeling they were making me think it through, so it would be my own decision.

"The red female, Eshshah," I said, "she is the missing lady's dragon, is she not?"

I caught a flinch from Calder, but he answered my question in the affirmative.

"Do you think the dragon or her rider would mind greatly if she could keep in contact with me while I'm inside? I mean, this would only be with her consent and your opinion that her lady would not object."

"That is a very good suggestion, Amáne," Braonán said. "I believe Eshshah would be ... fine with that proposition and I am willing to wager, her rider would as well."

Avano added, "It's an option we'll have to discuss with the

Healer to see if she anticipates any danger to you or Eshshah, but I'm sure she'll agree to let us try."

I gritted my teeth and convinced myself that having her voice in my head would add to the success of our operation. That is if I could even understand her noise. As soon as I set the explosions and met up with Braonán, I would ask her to stop.

Chapter Twenty-One

Braonán, Avano and I headed toward the field where Eshshah and Sovann rested. They told me they had spoken with the Healer. She'd voiced a bit of apprehension, but did give permission for me to attempt thought transference with Eshshah.

We approached the red dragon, closer than I would have felt comfortable had I been on my own. I felt her warm breath and caught her intriguing scent. Spicy. Pleasant, with a hint of, *what is that? Campfire? Yes, or a hearth fire.* It inspired comfort. My fear of her lessened.

The three of us saluted. Eshshah nodded in response. I followed Avano and Braonán's example and saluted Sovann as well. He was quite a bit more intimidating. Sovann signaled his acknowledgment before lowering his great head and curling back around himself to resume his slumber.

I assumed for my benefit Avano spoke aloud to Eshshah. "Fiery Eshshah, our greetings to you. As you know, at dawn we'll begin our sortie against Galtero. Amáne has seen the advantage of thought transference and wanted to ask your permission to communicate with her while she's in the castle."

Her golden eyes lit up. If a dragon could smile, her reaction was exactly what I would have imagined. I read an excitement in them. They whirled.

"The Healer has some concerns," Avano added, before he became silent. By the look on his face, I suspected he spoke in secret to Eshshah.

I frowned at being left out of the conversation.

Avano turned to me. "Eshshah's eager to give this a try. Are you ready?"

His eyes moved to my hands. "Relax. Stop making fists. This isn't going to hurt. She'll merely speak with you, just like I'm talking to you, now. There's nothing to fear."

I nodded.

I'm as ready as I can be, not knowing what to expect.

Turning to Eshshah, I said, "Please fiery dragon, talk to me."

I steeled myself. For what? I didn't know.

Silence. But, more than that, there was an absence of sound, as if all noise had been sucked out of existence. The edges of my sight dimmed, then darkness closed in. My heart accelerated. A sound like metal against metal reached my ears. At first distant and muted, it began to crescendo. Before I could cry out in alarm, an explosion went off in my head. I gripped my temples and squeezed my eyes shut as lightning lit the insides of my eyelids. Falling to my knees, I brought my head to the ground and screamed in pain.

Then, just as suddenly, a calmness fell. Only the sound of my breath echoed in short gasps. Avano and Braonán stooped down next to me. Avano rolled me over and cradled me in his arms.

"Amáne?" Fear seized his voice.

"I ... I'm alright. I think. It appears I failed the test," I said through a forced smile.

Braonán groaned. "I hope we didn't just make a grave mistake."

"Wh ... what are you saying? Would what just happened have an effect against getting my memories back?" I swallowed my panic.

"I don't know ..." he said. "Let's hope this didn't mar your chances of a full recovery."

I stifled a sob.

Eshshah's large head came close. Her eyes dulled with distress.

"Eshshah," I said out loud. "Please, don't trouble yourself. It was not anything you did. It was me. I'm not a dragon rider, so now we've proven I wouldn't be able to communicate with you as if I were one."

I turned and glared at Braonán, "As to regaining my past, I am not giving up hope." My voice ended in a whisper.

Eshshah hummed as she breathed on me. The last of my pain disappeared.

Avano gathered his arms around me as if to pick me up.

"No, no, please. I'm fine. Don't carry me. I can walk." I pushed him away.

"Stubborn girl," I heard under his breath. But he moved back, rose to his feet and offered me his hand. I let him help me up.

I faced Eshshah and said, "Thank you, I know it was your doing that my pain has been relieved. You have a beautiful gift of healing and I'm grateful you shared it with me."

She tipped her head.

I offered her a genuine smile. Her eyes brightened a bit. Forgetting any previous fear, I reached my hand out to her. She lowered her head and touched it with her nose. We remained in that posture for a brief moment. I found myself almost in love with this great creature.

Maybe I wouldn't mind becoming a dragon rider one day. That is, if I can be assured of linking to a dragon like her.

"I have an idea." I swung my eyes to Braonán and Avano. My heart beat lighter. "It appears Eshshah can understand me fine when I speak to her, so what if we make do with a one-way contact? I can use the open thought transference — just me communicating with her. If we're able to at least make that work, then I can keep you apprised of my whereabouts in the castle."

"Brilliant idea, Amáne," Braonán said. "But after what you've just undergone, we will not be doing any such experiments."

My shoulders dropped. "What? You're willing to just give up in finding a way for me to communicate? This is an important part of the success of the mission. It would be different than her communicating with me. I feel in my heart it will work."

The two held fast. Their lips pressed in a straight line.

I stomped my foot in exasperation. "Please let me try. There's not much time left. I'd feel better knowing I'll have some way to stay in contact with you riders. Don't you see how important this is?"

"We do see that, Amáne," Avano said.

He rubbed his forehead with one hand and dragged it down his face, stopping at his chin. "Let's see what the Healer says about it. She needs to know what happened here. Mind you, if she opposes for any reason, we won't go through with it. We will not jeopardize your healing. Any more than we already may have." He uttered the last part as if to himself.

I pursed my lips.

Chapter Twenty-Two

I waited in the dining hall while Avano and Braonán proceeded to the ante room with the communication device. After several minutes, Avano asked me to enter. Braonán stood before the glass, the Healer's reflection filled the disc. Concern showed on her face.

My heart sank.

I have to do something before she denies my request.

I concentrated on a vision of me standing before Eshshah and speaking to her. Placing my hand in front of my mouth, I whispered with all my heart, "Eshshah, if you can hear me, please tell Avano. Please, Eshshah, can you hear me?"

Avano's head snapped around. Our eyes locked. I shot him an innocent smile.

"What is it Avano?" the Healer said.

Not bothering to hide my mouth, I said in a low voice, "Eshshah, thank you. Tell him I feel no pain, or anything similar to what I'd experienced earlier. He can inform the Healer we have communication for our mission."

"Healer," Avano said. His eyes darted to mine before he turned back to the image in the glass. "It appears Amáne has taken it upon herself to test her theory with Eshshah. Eshshah can hear her, and Amáne appears to be unaffected."

The Healer's eyebrows came together.

"Amáne?" she said.

I stepped up in front of the glass and cringed at her expression. *Could she still forbid me to talk to Eshshah? She is certainly a woman of power, but...*

I saluted. "Yes, Lady Healer?"

She took a moment to compose herself, but did not hide the sternness in her voice. "Please do not play lightly with your ... condition. There's an important aspect to your situation that you don't understand. It would be to all of our advantage if you would heed the warnings you're given. While I'm pleased to hear you can communicate with Eshshah, your disregard for our caution is not appreciated."

Thoroughly abashed, I said, "My apologies, Lady Healer. You're right, I don't understand."

Her voice softened. "Amáne, understand this: we have your best interest in mind, but it goes much further than your interest alone. Your health has more far-reaching implications. You must accept that truth."

"I do, Lady Healer."

She exhaled. "Since you've already proven some success, you may continue your experiments. But if you feel the slightest pain or doubt, abandon your test."

I dipped my head. "Thank you, Lady Healer."

Her attention shifted to Braonán for a few more words before they signed off.

Once the Healer's image faded from the disc, Avano turned to me with his head tilted and a reprimanding set to his mouth. He may as well have said "Tsk tsk tsk" out loud.

I shrugged my shoulders, and said, "At least we know it works."

"Then, we may as well start testing the distance," he said.

We moved to another location in the inn, increasing our range.

"Very good," said Avano. "She heard you again. Now try it without saying it out loud."

"You mean talk to her in my mind?"

He nodded.

I scrunched my eyes shut and inwardly said, "Eshshah, how about now?" My lips still moved.

Avano burst out laughing. "She heard you, but you didn't have to make it look so painful. And, I could read your lips like you were shouting. You don't have to squeeze your eyes closed like that, either. Try to look normal."

I scowled. "Look, you've been doing this for countless years. It comes naturally to you. I'm still trying to get used to the thought of dragons even existing, let alone being able to talk to one."

I held his eyes in my glare as I mentally said, "Eshshah please tell this annoying man to step back and show a little more compassion. He has no idea what it's like for me and he appears to not give a care. I'm done practicing for the night. I wish you a pleasant sleep. But for this rider, I wish him a stone in his mattress."

Avano's eyes opened wide. I couldn't hold my smirk. He threw his head back and laughed loudly.

"Bravo, Amáne. You are now a thought transference expert."

"Even if it's only a one-way conveyance," I grumbled.

"Come with me. I know you hoped you were done for the night. It is late, but let's try one more distance before I retire for an uncomfortable rest. Truthfully? A stone in my mattress?"

I tipped a shoulder up.

He clapped me on the back and strode out of the inn. I rushed to keep pace with him.

"Where are we going? This better not take long, Avano. You're forgetting our mission begins at dawn."

"*Your* mission begins at dawn. I don't fly until nightfall."

"Ugh. You are impossible," I laughed. "If I were your queen, I'd command, 'Off with your head.'"

He missed a step as I kept walking.

I turned to look back at him and couldn't decipher his odd expression. "What?"

"This way," he said.

Avano led me to a dragon. A grey. "Amáne, I would like you to meet my dragon, Arai. Her name means 'cloud.' Arai please meet Amáne."

She dipped her head low as I saluted her and said, "Greetings, Arai, may your flame never extinguish."

Avano began to check his dragon's tack, tightening her girth and inspecting the straps.

"What are you doing?" I asked.

"She still has the double saddle on. We're going on a ride."

I gasped. "Oh, oh, oh, no! I'm not flying on a dragon."

"We need to do one more test, this time at a real distance."

"It would make much more sense if Eshshah goes on the flight and I keep my feet on the ground."

"I disagree," he said as he hoisted himself into the saddle and held his hand down to me.

"I ... I'm afraid of heights ... I think."

"I have the feeling you're not afraid of much."

"What about the Healer. She might not ..."

"I've already cleared it with her."

"You're going to make me get on that dragon, aren't you?"

A corner of his mouth lifted.

Black Castle

I closed my eyes and breathed out.

How did I ever get into this?

Maybe it was pride or maybe part of my identity, but something in me surfaced. I would not show cowardice. There would be no backing down. With determination, I climbed on Arai's foreleg, reached up and locked wrists with Avano. Planting one foot on the footpeg, I pulled myself up and swung my leg over the back of the saddle.

Avano helped me with the two straps that came up in the middle of the saddle and buckled over my thighs. He handed me a helmet that looked like the same one I'd worn when we sparred. Reaching for the small lever at my temple, he lowered the protective lenses for me.

"You ready?" he said.

With my teeth clenched, I said, "No."

"Hold on."

I wrapped my arms around his waist and buried my forehead in his back.

"You can loosen your grip if you don't mind."

I squeezed tighter.

I felt Arai's powerful muscles contract as she gathered her hind legs under her. She opened her expansive wings and thrust off the ground. One powerful downward pump and we shot skyward.

I screamed. Avano laughed.

The steady beat of Arai's wings eased my fear. I relaxed my hold, but left my hands clasped around Avano's waist. Slowly, I opened my eyes, keeping them directed at his back.

His dragon spiraled higher. When my pulse reached a more normal rate, I drew my gaze to my right.

I gasped as I caught sight of the indigo sky filled with stars. It was as if I were a part of the thousand lights dotting the celestial dome around me. A laugh shot straight from my heart. Before I could hold back I let out a whoop of sheer joy.

Sitting up straight, I let go of Avano and threw my arms in the air.

"This is nothing short of glorious," I shouted over the wind.

Avano's laughter blew back to me as the air currents whipped my clothes.

"See if Eshshah can hear you," he said.

After a pause, he relayed she heard me clearly.

"Eshshah, won't you join us? It's beautiful and peaceful up here. I couldn't have imagined this would be so awe-inspiring."

No longer afraid, I glanced down. The emerald island grew smaller beneath us. I spotted a small red object heading our way from below. It grew until I recognized Eshshah's form.

She leveled out next to us as she and Arai soared wing to wing. Her magnificent glistening scales gave the impression she glowed. Embers in a fire.

"You're beautiful, Eshshah," I said out loud.

Her golden eye turned toward me. For one split moment a reflection in it made me sad. She blinked and it was gone. In the next breath, she peeled off, diving to the right. Arai followed. After my stomach returned, I realized they were playing a game. I screamed in delight as the two dove and glided in the updrafts. I could have stayed up there all night, but Avano's voice brought me out of my musing.

"It's time to head back."

A cold reality froze in my chest. At dawn I would begin the mission for which we had been planning. I sobered instantly.

Chapter Twenty-Three

I tossed and thrashed through most of the night, tangled in my bedding. Bloodied swords, fiery projectiles and an evil presence in a black robe invaded my dreams. I bolted upright. My eyes frantically searched for the threat, but I found myself alone and presumably safe in a bed. It took some moments to remember where I was. When my trembling subsided, I lay back down, only to face the same scenes. My nightmares woke me several times.

The night dragged on. Dawn couldn't come soon enough. At last, the day's first light filtered into my room. I rubbed my burning eyes, leaped out of bed and grabbed the clothes Mora'ina had left for me. They were similar to what the dragon riders wore. With shaking hands I donned a pair of dark tights and a loose shirt of the same dark color. Before I could pull on a black tunic of a lightweight fabric, Mora'ina entered carrying a leather breastplate.

Holding it toward me, she said, "Amáne must put next, then that." She pointed at the tunic I held. "This have scale of dragon. Keep Amáne safe."

The breastplate was the same I had used the day before. Beautifully hand-tooled leather, oiled and soft, with dragon scales between the outer and inside layers. I gladly accepted it. Mora'ina helped secure it on before I slipped into the tunic.

I met the riders in the common room and forced myself, at Braonán's insistence, to put something in my stomach. Closing my eyes, I willed it to stay down.

We made our way to the supply cart and the crate in which I would be smuggled into the castle. My palms wouldn't stay dry, no matter how many times I wiped them on my tunic. Sweat trickled down my back, and not only because of the humidity.

Relief washed over me when Braonán said I didn't have to be sealed in the crate just yet. I could sit with the driver until we were closer to the castle. The trek would take almost two hours. The last half hour of which I would ride in the box.

My hand gripped the hilt of my sword so no one would see it shake. All the dragon riders at the inn, about a dozen, gathered to see me off. They offered various versions of well wishes. Their moods were uplifting. Some gave me a hardy clap on the back. Others joked to make the situation lighter. A few bowed with a respect I didn't understand.

Acknowledging their greetings with a nod or a forced smile, I hoped they couldn't see through my brave façade.

Avano stepped up to me. "Here's one more item you may need. It's a potion from the Healer. It helps to rejuvenate and give you energy. I wish we had more. This is the last of it." He handed me a small vial filled with a dark liquid. "Put it in this pouch and hang it on your belt."

"Is that the horrible stuff Mora'ina made me drink?" I made a face.

"Yes, the same. You'll overlook the taste when you have need to use it."

BLACK CASTLE

I reached for the container and couldn't hide my trembling hand.

Avano placed the vial in the pouch for me and attached it to my belt. Then he rested his hands on my shoulders and pressed down. Surprisingly, this had a somewhat calming effect.

"Amáne, stop pretending you're not nervous. You're not doing that great of a job hiding it anyway."

I threw him a dark look.

"You need to know we understand. We've all been through dozens of missions like this. Some of the older riders have been through hundreds. You wouldn't be human if you didn't have some anxiety. We're all with you. It'll be over before you know it. We'll see you tonight. As soon as the first explosion goes off, we'll take flight. The dragons from the Valley of Dragons have offered their assistance. It should be quite a spectacular showing." He smiled.

My spirits lifted. I turned to the group. "I'll see you all by break of day tomorrow. I'm looking forward to meeting your king."

Out of the corner of my eye, I saw Avano's face twitch. Several riders looked away quickly.

The supply wagon journeyed through the jungle on a narrow cart path. Frequent rains left the road in poor condition. The donkey had no way around the ruts and stones. My teeth jarred with every pothole as I sat with the driver, thankful I didn't have to endure the entire trip in the crate.

My stomach lurched when the cart stopped. The driver looked at me and nodded. I closed my eyes, swallowed and returned his nod. We didn't speak the same language, but we were in complete understanding.

Climbing to the back of the cart, I lowered myself into the straw-lined crate. I curled on my side and lay in a fetal position, adjusting my sword in its scabbard so the driver could fit the lid on the crate. My boots hid a set of daggers. Once I reached the castle, I would retrieve my glaive and bow.

Taking a deep jagged breath, I indicated to the driver I'd settled.

The man fitted the top and proceeded to nail it shut. My anxiety grew. I took in several quick gasps.

The cart driver stopped hammering and said something.

Even in another language, I felt his concern. "I'm alright. Go ahead and finish."

He drove in a few more nails as I gained control of my panic. The boards allowed in small slivers of light, as well as air. It helped ease my fear of the confined space.

The road became even more unbearable. As we bounced along, I occupied my mind by going over some fight sequences Avano had shown me. With eyes closed, I mentally went through the steps and thrusts of my sword and my glaive.

My muscles complained at having to remain in the same cramped position. Small adjustments were all I could manage.

The supply cart at last came to a halt. I heard talking and whispering of several people in the now-familiar native tongue.

I braced myself at the sensation of my crate being lifted off the wagon. The men carrying me adjusted the weight as I jostled inside. Then the ride smoothed out and I swayed with their strides. The first leg of this undertaking into the castle would soon be over and I could pour myself into my mission. My whole body itched with anticipation that I'd soon be free of this claustrophobic crate.

The motion of my container halted.

We've reached the kitchen already? I expected it to be a bit farther.

Black Castle

Cries of consternation reached my ears. My senses were alerted. Heavy bootsteps sounded around me.

"We're inspecting the supplies," a rough voice declared.

A fear I could almost taste bit me.

No, this can't be happening. They weren't supposed to be checking for another day or two.

My hand gripped the hilt of my sword so hard it hurt.

"Put that crate down, an' all you savages stand over there."

A downward sensation and then a jolt told me my transporters had complied with the command.

I felt a rap against the box. Something metal struck the side.

"What's in here?" a man said. Another thump shook the box. This time lower, like a boot.

"For King. King want," said a female voice with the same accent as Mora'ina.

"I said, what's in here?"

"Special. Food from ocean. Need in kitchen soon. To cook. It rot fast. King be very angry."

"Open it."

Silence.

A thud, like a fist on flesh, then a yelp.

"I told ya ta open it."

Shuffling feet and scared voices sounded from one direction, a short distance away. My muscles tightened, adrenaline flowed through my body. I breathed in and breathed out slowly as I tried to gather my wits for what I'd hoped would not happen.

An object struck the top of my crate several times. Between the lid and the walls of the crate a metal bar worked its way in. The wood creaked and splintered as the lid was torn off.

Ignoring my screaming muscles, I leaped up and out, brandishing my sword. The closest guard went down easily. The native who'd pried off the top dropped to his hands and knees, trying to avoid the fight. I spun and lunged at the next guard as he drew his sword. It was half unsheathed when I ran him through. My hopes fell when several large men charged at me, halberds raised.

"Keep 'er alive," shouted one particularly burly man.

I remained frozen in a fighting stance, my lips pulled back in defiance. But there was little hope of escape.

The soldiers surrounded me. The tips of their poleaxes inches from my face.

"Go ahead," said the burly man. "Gimme a excuse to bloody my blade."

I glared at him. He moved his weapon closer to my cheek. I held my position, hoping they couldn't hear my heart pound in my chest. The man pulled the spike at the end of his halberd across my cheekbone. Trying not to flinch, I clenched my teeth as warm blood ran down my face.

The man barked out a laugh as he pulled his weapon back. "Welcome back. The king's gonna be real excited to see ya again, tho' he ain't gonna be happy ya killed two o' his." He eyed the dead soldiers. "Yer a tough lil' lady, but don' be stupid. Drop yer sword. Now."

Red hot anger rose in my throat. I swallowed it back.

He's right.

My shoulders slumped. I couldn't afford to be careless. Not while there was still hope of staying alive.

This mission cannot fail — failure is not an option.

I bent over and placed my sword on the ground.

He laughed. "That's a smart little warrior, showin' care for yer weapon. Now kick it out of the way."

I shoved it away with my foot.

Black Castle

Three men moved in and grabbed my arms. They yanked my hands behind me and slapped manacles on my wrists.

It's like they expected my arrival.

I glared at the natives around me to see if I could find a guilty face. But they all stood in horror as the guards led me away. Another tribesman stood in a nearby doorway watching. He spun around and slinked back inside when I caught his eye.

My stomach twisted violently. Sweat soaked my shirt.

CHAPTER TWENTY-FOUR

The metal-barred door clanged shut and the bolt fell into place. I sat on the dirt floor with my wrists locked in irons at my back. A quick look about was all I needed to survey my small cell and the damp walls that enclosed me.

The echo of doors slammed down the corridor. I imagined the natives captured with me found themselves in similar surroundings.

My captors passed my cell, heading back the way we had come. One of the guards, with long greasy hair, slowed his pace and leered as he passed. I nearly retched.

I waited until their bootsteps faded down the corridor.

Now's my chance to test Aperio's key.

Bending my wrist around the irons, I bit my lip at the pain of the metal pressing against my flesh. I persevered until I withdrew the dragonscale key from the hidden pocket in my sleeve.

Bootsteps echoed in the passageway. I froze. Someone headed back toward my cell. Palming the key, I listened and watched the cell door.

The greasy-haired guard who'd eyed me earlier, slipped into sight outside my cell. His lips turned up in a sickening sneer, an evil glint lit his eye. Letting himself in, he closed the cell door behind him. He took slow deliberate steps toward me. I scooted away until my back pressed against the wall.

"Ya don' remember ol' Gahn, do ya?"

He laughed. "Ah, yer still feelin' that fall 'int ya?"

I stood up.

"Well then, let me tell ya where we left off. Ya was 'bout ready to show me how much ya loved me."

Gahn moved in close, his stinking body pushed against mine. He gripped my jaw in his filthy hand and leaned in. I tried to turn my face away, but he held tight.

Behind my back, I frantically worked the key into the lock on the manacles.

"Aperio," I whispered.

He stopped before his lips reached my mouth.

"Wud ya say?"

"I said, Aperio." My voice raised in defiance. The manacles slid off my wrists and became my weapon.

Mentally, I reached for Eshshah. A surge of strength flowed into my body, seemingly from out of nowhere.

Eshshah?

I shook off my surprise at the intensity of power, then gathered myself and swung my iron-covered fists up into the miscreant's chin. The lecherous look on his face dropped. He flew backwards, landing hard on his back.

As he gasped for air, I leaped toward him and yanked the sword from his scabbard.

I spun away and faced him, raising the sword. But I hesitated.

Fear, then anger swept across his features. Before I could strike, he was swift to his feet, drawing a dagger in a fluid motion.

He slashed at me. I slid to the side and parried.

Gahn continued his advance, jabbing and slicing. The space was small. With his dagger, he fought too close for me to make any offensive moves with the sword. I kept up my defense, evading and blocking his shots.

At last I achieved some distance and found an opening. Before he could thrust again, I sliced my blade across his face. He stumbled. I wasted no time running the blade through his throat. Warm blood spattered on me.

My chest rose and fell in shallow rasping breaths. I swallowed the nausea that rose from my stomach as I stared at his body. No emotion moved in me.

I wiped my blade on the man's tunic. Trying to avoid looking directly at his staring eyes, I removed his sword belt and wrapped it around me. Sheathing the sword, I grabbed his dagger from the ground where it had dropped. A hasty search of his body procured another knife. With the knives stashed in my belt, I rushed to the cell door. Aperio's key opened the bars and I slid out. Assured I was alone in the corridor, I leaned against the wall to pull myself together.

"Eshshah," I whispered, "I'm all right. I'm going to see if I can help the others before I figure out where the guards have taken my weapons."

The corridor held more cells like the one I'd just escaped. Those I passed were empty. Whispering voices came from down the hall and drew me farther. With caution, I inched my way to the last cell and found the natives that had been captured with me. They leaned against the bars of their cell, craning their necks to get a glimpse in my direction. The clashing of weapons with Ghan had, no doubt, attracted their attention.

Black Castle

When I reached their door, they fell to their knees.

I shook my head in confusion and bid them to stand. Using Aperio's key I opened their cell door and one by one released them from their irons.

A native girl stepped up to me.

"Amáne." She took both of my hands and pressed them against her forehead.

"Do I know you?"

"Lia'ina." She put her hand on her chest, a questioning look in her eyes.

"You're Lia'ina?" I said.

She nodded. "Ah," she said in an understanding tone. "Manu'eno say Amáne lost mind."

"I didn't lose my mind," I snapped at her. "I lost my memory."

"Meh-mo-rhee?"

I huffed. "Never mind, yes, I lost my mind. You were the dragon riders' contact, weren't you?" She nodded. "Why do you act like you know me?"

She waved her hand in dismissal and said, "Teku'eno,"

"I'm sorry, I don't speak your language."

"Teku'eno betray Amáne. He tell evil lady you come in box."

He must have been the one I saw sneaking away.

"Teku'eno shame tribe. Soon he die for his bad." A frightening scowl twisted her face.

She closed her eyes and released a slow breath. Her anger in check, she said, "Not time to talk. Fast. We must go."

She pulled me out to the corridor. Her companions surrounded me in a protective shield. I handed the dagger to her and the knife to one of the men. I kept the sword.

Moving in silence, we took a route that led us to an upper level. Thus far, it seemed our escape hadn't been discovered as we ducked into an empty chamber. We needed a plan. Ten of us sneaking through the castle would be folly. I'd intended to free them and continue on alone, but I couldn't just leave them behind.

As if Lia'ina read my thoughts, she turned to me and whispered, "Too many. Not safe. Is long hole under dirt in castle. Lead to big water by mountain." She bit her lip in frustration. "Ancestors make hole. Lia'ina look and look, but not find. So sorry. Many men watch doors. Lia'ina must find other out."

"No need to be sorry, I know where the tunnel is. I can show you."

Her eyes went wide.

I moved to a nearby table and drew some lines in the dust. I'd studied the castle floorplans enough to figure out where we stood and how to get to the old kitchen where Braonán said the tunnel was located.

The group paid close attention. They each gave an indication they understood where they needed to go.

"You can separate and go in three groups." I held up three fingers. "Three, three and three."

Lia'ina shook her head. "Not three, three, three. Four, three, three." She flashed the corresponding number of fingers.

I shook my head, "I have to stay and finish my work."

"No. Amáne must go. Be safe."

"I can't go with you, Lia'ina," I said firmly. "There's a job I've come to do. First, I have to find the weapons and equipment that came here with me. Then I need to continue my mission."

She started to object, but I interrupted her. "I cannot shame my tribe, Lia'ina. I must complete my task."

Her eyes reflected understanding. She smiled and said, "Lia'ina go with Amáne." She pointed first at herself, then at me.

Black Castle

Before I could respond, a member of her tribe confronted her. He seemed to have understood her intention. Although she was the tribal chief's daughter, the way he spoke to her demonstrated some authority. The conversation became heated. Their voices were low whispers, but the force of their words would not have been more powerful if they had shouted them.

Lia'ina huffed, then slumped. She gave a reluctant bob of her head.

Her eyes met mine as she said, "Lia'ina father tribal chief. He meet ancestors. Now Lia'ina chief. Must be safe for tribe. Not can go with Amáne." Her angry eyes darted toward the man with whom she'd argued. "Ramu'eno go. He find what Amáne seek. Then Ramu'eno must make Teku'eno pay. End him."

Chapter Twenty-Five

Ramu'eno motioned me behind him as he glanced up and down a corridor. Lia'ina and her tribesmen had already set off in three groups, leaving me with the native. I'd let Eshshah know of their escape, so someone could meet them on the north shore and take them to safety.

Not knowing each other's language, Ramu'eno and I communicated with pantomime gestures. Seeing the corridor was empty, Ramu'eno waved me on. We traveled down the hall soundlessly. From what I knew of the castle layout, we headed toward the working kitchen.

We arrived at a doorway. Ramu'eno bid me wait in the corridor as he slipped into the room. I peered around the corner and noted a single native, dressed in the same work clothes as Lia'ina and her companions. He stood at a table with his back facing us. The kitchen was otherwise empty.

Ramu'eno crept up behind him. He reached out with both hands and grabbed the man's head. His fingers wrapped around and dug into his eye sockets. Using them as a fingerhold, with a lightening move, he jumped up and to the side, pulling the man down and back hard, slamming his head on the ground before he had a chance to cry out. I stifled my gasp at the sound of the dull thud as his skull hit the stone floor. Blood oozed out of his eyes.

Ramu'eno jerked his head to me to join him in the kitchen, then signaled another wordless instruction to open a door to my left.

He dragged the unconscious man into a small pantry and I closed the door behind us. Taking his knife, he cut pieces of the native's shirt, tied his hands and feet and secured a gag over his mouth. While he worked, he indicated the man was Teku'eno.

Ramu'eno spread his hand out to me to wait there while he slid out the door. He returned moments later with a bowl of water that he poured on Teku'eno's face. The captive native sputtered and coughed as he regained consciousness. His face twisted with fear. He struggled against the bonds.

Ramu'eno's face turned vicious as he dropped to his knee on the traitor's chest. Air forced out of the man's lungs. He struggled to take in a breath.

Holding his knife to the downed man's throat, Ramu'eno spat venomous words at Teku'eno, who lay powerless under him. Ramu'eno loosened the gag and pressed harder with the knife, coercing the man to talk.

A series of angry words were exchanged, but in moments Teku'eno's defiance waned. Ramu'eno's voice became lower and more ominous. If Lia'ina hadn't expressed confidence in his loyalty, I would have been in fear of Ramu'eno, myself.

Stifling a yelp, I watched in horror as Ramu'eno pulled his knife across the man's throat. His own tribesman. Blood spurted, then pooled beneath him. Ramu'eno wiped the blade on Teku'eno's shirt before rising to his feet. A fierce look distorted his face as he continued his rant directed at the body.

Should I have trusted Lia'ina's assurance about this man?

My hand went to the sword at my side.

Ramu'eno noted my action. He immediately shook his head and made a great show of slipping his knife in his belt. He held up both hands as if in surrender and spoke quickly in his own language. His tone was that of reassurance. I studied him for several seconds before I relaxed my grip on my sword.

He nodded and beckoned me to follow.

He must have gotten the information he needed from Teku'eno.

I hoped the dead man's last words were spoken to redeem himself.

We stole through several corridors, all fortunately empty, until we came to a low wooden door. Ramu'eno tried the latch. It was locked. I signaled him aside as I drew Aperio's key. Placing the key in the lock, I whispered, "Aperio," and the latch released.

Ramu'eno jerked back and eyed the key suspiciously.

"Dragon scale," I said, over-pronouncing my words as I held it for him to see.

He dipped his head and then snapped back to our task at hand. We ducked through the door. A weapons supply room. My eyes took in the multitude of swords, shields, knives and spears. I scanned the space and exhaled a triumphant "yes" as I spotted my glaive, sword, daggers and bow, all stacked in one corner. I could, however, only find two of my three blast sticks. My stomach sank.

I'll have to succeed with only two.

That would leave one harpoon cannon intact.

Tossing Gahn's inferior sword, I pulled on my sword belt, sheathed my belt dagger and my boot daggers, then grabbed my bow and glaive. I slipped my quiver of arrows with Eshshah's embedded scales, over my shoulder, and pulled on my dragonscale scull cap helmet. Ramu'eno picked a few choice daggers and slid them into his belt.

Black Castle

We headed back to the old north kitchen where the escape tunnel lay. Ramu'eno helped me drag a work table aside to expose the trap door beneath. I pulled it open for him and pantomimed my thanks, bidding him to go and find his tribesmen. He put his hand on my back and guided me to the tunnel entrance, gesturing for me to enter before him.

Shaking my head and speaking partly with my hands, I said slowly, "I have to wait here until dark. I will see you tomorrow."

I hope.

Ramu'eno tipped his head in understanding. He held out his hand, which I took in a firm grip. Bringing it to his forehead, he bowed to me, then turned and disappeared into the dark tunnel. Closing the trap door behind him, I pushed the table back over it and then sat on the floor to await my moment.

CHAPTER TWENTY-SIX

Sitting idle, just waiting, made me anxious and impatient. My mind raced with a swarm of questions.

Who is the real Amáne? How do I know how to fight? Am I a mercenary? An assassin for hire?

I couldn't have been a bad person. The dragon riders knew my past. I didn't think they would so readily take me in if I'd been evil.

Would they?

Unless they needed me only for this mission, and then planned to dismiss me. By that time, I hoped my memories would have returned.

To calm my nerves and pass the time, I started to count. I made it to one thousand, then stopped and counted backwards from there. It helped only a bit, not enough. Before I fell into a black mood, I decided to contact Eshshah. She gave me such comfort. I envied her rider.

"Eshshah? If you're listening, I'm sorry to bother you, but I need someone to talk to. I'm tired of talking to myself."

I told her how I'd found my weapons and that I'd said farewell to Ramu'eno. He should be arriving at the north shore within the half hour.

BLACK CASTLE

My rambling one-way conversation went on. I couldn't help thinking about the missing lady.

"Eshshah, I hope your rider knows how lucky she is to have you. I wonder why it is that you can't communicate with her. If King Ansel's dragon can be in contact with him, why can't you find her?"

I realized what I said may have upset Eshshah.

What if her rider has met with her ancestors?

That would certainly be a reason for the absence of contact. If that were the case, then they would be anxious to find her body and take her home.

I'll volunteer to hunt for the lady, or her body, until she's found.

My conversing with Eshshah didn't have the uplifting effect in which I'd hoped. I spiraled down into my dark thoughts.

A commotion in the corridor brought me out of my darkness.

"Someone is coming, Eshshah."

I leaped to my feet and sprinted toward a nearby door. Pulling on the knob, I found it locked. The bootsteps grew louder. I yanked Aperio's key from my sleeve and whispered the dragon's name. The latch clicked. The door opened. Another storage closet. I rushed in and shut it behind me as silently as I could. Whispering 'Aperio' once again, the bolt fell into place, locking me inside.

Thankfully, I had pushed the work table back over the trap door. I prayed they wouldn't discover it.

"If we don' find her, Galtero'll have our heads."

"Did you tell 'im, yet? That she's gone missin'?"

"Of course not, ya fool. An' he's not gonna know 'bout it neither. We're findin' 'er."

"Borit told me when Galtero heard she was back, he went purple. He swore he was personally gonna kill 'er along with that fancy lord. She goes first. He says he's gonna do it nice and slow so Drekinn could watch." He laughed.

My blood froze.

"If we can't find her, ya idiot, it's gonna be us instead. So, quit yer laughin' and start searchin'."

"Curse that Gahn. It's his fault she got away. Why can't he ever keep his hands to hisself? She was too much for 'im. Maybe she is bewitched."

"Well, he won't be botherin' nobody no more. She stuck 'im with his own blade. And him such a good fighter an' all. Yeah there's somethin' 'bout her. Maybe she got sorcery like Lady Ravana."

"Quit yer yappin'. Go check that closet."

I held my breath as I listened to the guard approach. The door knob giggled and then I heard him jerking and trying to work the lock. My glaive at the ready, I prepared to fight. The door held tight.

"It's locked," the man said with an added curse.

I stifled a cry when something struck the wood. Another smash hit the door, and another.

He's using his halberd to break down the door.

I steeled myself to attack.

"Wadda think yer doin'? Ya stupid or somethin'? That door's locked from the outside. Those doors don't lock from the inside. That means she ain't in there. Come on. We got a lot o' rooms to search."

I nearly collapsed with relief as the sound of their boots retreated. After a space of time had passed and I was certain they would not return, I unlocked the closet. Peering around the door, my eyes swept the room. It was safe to exit.

Trying to calm my shaking, I made my way slowly across the kitchen and sat with my back against a wall to resume my wait for nightfall.

BLACK CASTLE

I thought about the king. What if they hurt him because of my escape? Maybe after I ignite the blast sticks I should search for him.

How will I know if he makes his escape?

Too many variables. I didn't know what I should do.

Just continue with the plan, Amáne. That's all you can do.

A sigh of frustration passed my lips.

I jerked awake. A small tremor shook the ground beneath me.
What is that?

Just as quickly, the rumbling stopped and the ground stilled.
It must have been part of my dream.

Wide-eyed, I studied my surroundings. My heart slowed as I remembered where I was.

I'd been dreaming about falling off a cliff and being rescued by a fiery red dragon. In the dream, I fought a large man in black armor. Something about the nightmare haunted the back of my mind. I'd had this dream in the past. The fleeting memory faded before I could get a hold of it.

At last, night fell. The wait had ended. My nerves would soon calm as I prepared for my task. I breathed in deeply and let it out in a slow exhalation.

Pulling myself to my feet, I peered around a crumpled wall. This part of the old kitchen had been partially destroyed in a volcano. I stood on the north side which opened out onto a courtyard. Its cracked tiles had lost the fight against the overtaking jungle. Plants, vines and trees had reclaimed much of this side of the castle. This was to my advantage. It would provide some cover when I made my way toward the west exterior wall.

My glaive would be a hindrance as I completed the next step, so I hid it behind a work table to retrieve after I'd set the blast sticks. The sword sheathed at my side, I strung my bow and slid it over my shoulder. With a quiver full of arrows, I had all I needed.

I surveyed the route I planned to take. A quick glance in either direction assured my path was clear. I stepped out into the courtyard and turned left. In short dashes between the trees, I came to the final edge of the leafy screen.

Eyeing the harpoon cannon that sat atop the battlement, I pinpointed where I needed to set the first blast stick at the wall's stone base. The drain spout, just as Braonán had indicated on the map, protruded near the ground.

With one last deep breath, I said, "Eshshah, here I go."

Timing would be important for this last stretch across the unprotected part of the courtyard and the open area beyond. Keeping my eye on the guards that paced the wall walk, I gritted my teeth and darted across the exposed grounds.

The fountain Calder had mentioned stood in ruins at the farthest perimeter of the courtyard. As I ran by it, I decided the dragon rider was right. It could work as a strategic location from which to take my shots. Its distance from my targets would be within my range.

With a final burst of speed I reached my goal. My heart pounded as I leaned my back against the stones of the fortress' outer wall. Without waiting to catch my breath, I turned and removed the blast stick from where it hung on my belt. The drain spout jutting out from the wall was carved with a hideous face, part-animal, part-human. It's mouth open wide to belch out the rain water redirected from the wall walk above. Bending over the spout, I shoved the stick in the creature's mouth as deeply as I could, making sure the fuse remained exposed.

Black Castle

Braonán had told me from that point I needed to count my steps to where I'd find the push rock that would open a hidden passage into the exterior wall. I paced the advised distance and felt along the wall at the height he instructed.

After several moments of searching, my frustration grew. "Eshshah, I can't find it."

Should I go back and start counting again?

I pressed my hand to my forehead. *Think, Amáne, think. Had I miscounted or misheard the number?*

I'd already checked a second time a few paces in either direction without encountering the rock.

A flash of awareness hit me. The paces Braonán gave me were more likely the paces of a man, not one of my stature. It would stand to reason, I hadn't reached the location yet. With renewed hope, I continued along the wall. My hands sought the stone.

"It's here, Eshshah," I nearly shouted as my tension released.

I prayed the mechanism still worked as I pressed on the rock. And especially, that it would not make a sound that would draw attention. A slight rumble vibrated to my left. Stone against stone. Creaking and scraping. I cringed and held my breath, hoping no one could hear it, or feel it. A small crack opened and then widened to allow enough of an opening for me to slip inside. I found and pressed the push rock on that side. The stone door closed and I was left in darkness.

I waited for my eyes to adjust, but the shadows were deep. I could barely make out the silhouettes of ropes in front of me.

Why would there be ropes hanging inside the walls?

My eyes played tricks on me, making me think the ropes had stirred. There was no movement of air inside the stifling tunnel. The floor also seemed to shift beneath my feet. I drew my sword and swiped at the shapes. A muffled thud smacked the ground in front of me.

Something hit my arm and a pain shot through me. Another piercing strike, and another, and a last hit to my face.

My hands shaking from fear and pain, I reached for an arrow from my quiver. I fumbled with the leather receptacle at my back and managed to extract one.

"Eshshah," I whispered and a flame burst from the end of the shaft. The arrow became a torch. I held the light high in front of me.

"Snakes!" I shrieked.

Not just snakes, they were deadly vipers. I'd been struck several times. The reality of my situation hit me hard.

"Eshshah, I've failed. I'm sure to die inside these walls. I'm sorry."

The pain of the venom burned in my veins. I had difficulty breathing. My trauma brought to mind a similar experience. I'd endured a venomous bite before. Perhaps more than once. But like the other memories that had flashed through my mind, this one evaporated immediately.

I whispered Eshshah's name again to increase the size of the flame on the arrow. The tunnel brightened. The flame reflecting off the glistening scales of the snakes showed them everywhere — above and below me. One dropped on my shoulder, it's cold slick tail curled around my neck. I stifled a scream as I grabbed it and flung it against the wall.

I brandished my torch high and low, jabbing it at the serpents in my way. A path cleared as they slithered away from the light. My pain was intense, but so far I'd kept to my feet. I persevered, determined to at least set the second blast stick. Hopefully, one of the dragon riders would be able to ignite them. I could at least do that much to help the king.

Black Castle

A familiar surge of power flowed through me. "Eshshah, I know that's you. If I could complete my task, I would be eternally grateful."

I fought my way through the sea of snakes, scattering them before me. On the edge of hysteria, I lost track of my location inside the wall. But a turn in the passage told me I'd arrived at the next site. Finding the push rock, I pressed it. The door responded to my request. It opened slowly. Cautiously, I stuck my head out once the opening became large enough. Scanning the grounds, I saw my way was clear. Before the door opened fully, I slipped through and quickly found and pressed the lever to close it behind me.

Shivering with relief, I inhaled fresh air. I'd made it out of that tunnel. My outlook improved, but the snakebites may yet be my end. I had to work quickly before the venom overcame me.

Wary of my surroundings, I scanned the base of the wall and found the drain spout where I would place the second blast stick.

Squatting in front of yet another grotesque carved figure that projected from the wall, I forced the blast stick into its mouth, then extended the fuse to make it an accessible target for the igniting shot.

Although my pain radiated from the bites I'd sustained, the fact I could still function and that my body still responded to all that I asked of it, made no sense.

How could it be that the venom hadn't overcome me? Is Eshshah keeping me alive until I finish my mission?

A vision flickered at the outer edge of my consciousness — a hazy recollection of venom in my veins rose again, but still it remained at the edge.

My back to the wall, I surveyed my position to mark the course I'd take back to the fountain. It lay in ruins, but probably had been a magnificent structure when the castle was young. Now, its sections lay toppled and spread broken in the yard.

To my left, I had a clear view to the harpoon cannon under which I'd set the first blast stick. Turning to my right I could see the third cannon, that regrettably would not get destroyed, since my third stick had been confiscated.

I blinked as my attention drew more sharply in that direction. A commotion that took place atop the wall walk pulled my focus. A torch backlighted the scene. Several guards had gathered around one of their mates. He held up something up in his hand.

"Eshshah, it's my third blast stick."

Their animated movements conveyed a weighty discussion occurring. Raised voices, although indecipherable, carried an angry tone on the breeze. The man holding the stick jerked it up as another grabbed at it.

This is my chance.

Instantly, I pulled an arrow from my quiver and nocked it. This would be an impossible shot, but I needed to try. In one fluid motion I raised my bow and drew back slowly until my fingers anchored at the corner of my mouth. I inhaled and aimed. Imagining the arrow making its way to the fuse, I let my breath out slowly, ready to release the string.

Pushing and shoving ensued up on the walk. A guard blocked my target. My opportunity passed. I eased the string, releasing the tension, and lowered my bow. As I watched for another opportunity, someone made another grab for the stick and the holder again jerked it out of reach. This time he kept it held above him. My eyes went wide. He'd raised it too close to the torch. I let out a small gasp as I saw sparks jump over his head. As one, their movement stopped. They all focused on the blast stick. An unmistakable star-shaped fire worked its way down the fuse.

Black Castle

I didn't wait to see them jump to action, but took off running toward safety. The blast went off, shaking the ground below me. I made it to cover and slid, feet first, behind the fountain as pieces of rock and debris dropped around me.

Immediately, I rose to one knee. With my other leg extended straight out to my side, I sighted the gargoyle that held the second blast stick. Calling upon my concentration to block the screams and orders echoing from the battlements, I drew the bow back. With a vision of the arrow flying true, I loosed the shaft and whispered, "Eshshah" to light the dragonscale embedded in the arrow. I didn't move my bow or take a breath until it ignited.

Before the fuse burned far, I rolled to the other side of the broken fountain, came up on my knee and let fly a shot to the drain spout that held the first blast stick.

"Ugh!" It went wide.

Soldiers ran in every direction. Whipping out another arrow, I got it off at once. Keeping my eyes on the trajectory, I ducked in close to the fountain as blast number two sent stones, debris and bodies flying into the air.

I let out a cry of frustration. The force of the explosion had caused my arrow to veer, colliding with a soldier who'd run into its path. The point lodged in his thigh. As he fell, his head turned in my direction. He shouted and gestured toward me.

There was only time to loose one more arrow before I retreated. Paying no heed of being spotted, I stood, and with a self-control that surprised me I aimed, released the shaft and whispered Eshshah's name. Straightaway, I spun around and ran for the kitchen and the escape tunnel.

The percussion of the last blast stick sent tremors through the ground as I made it to the cover of the bushes and growth at the other end of the courtyard. A satisfied smile touched my lips.

Chapter Twenty-Seven

Chaos and confusion increased as roars and trumpeting filled the sky.

The dragons!

Outside the kitchen, I paused beside the crumbled wall to catch a quick glimpse of them. The frightful power of the winged beings overwhelmed me as they belched flames and dove in their attacks.

"Eshshah, I'm heading for the tunnel," I said as I rushed into the kitchen and made my way toward the escape hatch.

A noise behind me made me spin around.

I froze. Several people stood in the doorway on the other side of the room.

Galtero. His eyes met mine with an evil glare that sliced into my heart.

Accompanying him were three guards and a lady — the black-caped beauty I'd seen when I came out of the oubliette. I remembered her name as Ravana.

"Get her!" Galtero shouted at his guards.

My eyes darted right and left. There was no escape. I had to fight.

Black Castle

His three men-at-arms charged across the large room. The two in front wielded halberds, the third followed with a sword and shield. The soldier on the left had his weapon cocked back over his shoulder as he ran. Keeping up with him, the man on the right held the spear point of his poleaxe leveled at me.

"Eshshah, I need your strength," I said.

A surge of power rushed through me.

Diving for my glaive behind the work table where I'd hidden it, I rolled to my feet before they closed the distance. I pealed to my left as the first attacker swung. His aim went high. I ducked. The air swished over my head. Constantly moving to keep only that guard within reach, I shoved the butt end of my glaive between his legs and wrenched hard across his thigh. The man lurched and went down hard. His weapon flew forward. I plunged my blade into the back of his unarmored leg. He writhed on the floor as his blood pooled around him.

His death cries had little effect on me.

I maneuvered around the downed guard's body in an effort to trip up the second man. The move didn't work. His reach was long. I dodged the blade of his halberd. The glint in his eyes reflected his determination to end my life. My teeth clenched.

Not today, sir.

We exchanged a series of blows before I slid to his right.

Now's my chance.

I moved in close and brought my glaive over his right shoulder and behind him. Using it as a lever, I pushed forward on the top end of the staff and stuck my foot in front of him. He crashed to the floor, face first. I drove my blade through the base of his skull.

Breathing heavy, I turned my attention to my next attacker. He set upon me with his sword and shield. Leaping back, I opened the distance between us and thrust my glaive. He brought his shield down to block. Still backing and evading his strikes, I jabbed high. My opponent raised his shield up to parry. I executed another sequence of low then high strikes.

Ha, I have him trained and just where I need him.

I dropped my shoulder, feinting a low thrust. He lowered his shield. My glaive, still held high, I struck him in the throat. He fell. A huff of air forced from his lungs.

I must have been a mercenary or an assassin. Else why am I not feeling the emotion I should for three dead men? Had I been in so many battles, seen so much death, they're no longer people to me?

I shook off that horrid thought. Trying to catch my breath, I spun to face Galtero.

All through my fight with the three guards, I made an effort to stay aware of him, the woman and their location in the room. They had steered themselves almost at my back. Galtero drew his sword. Trying to even my breath, I crouched and readied my glaive.

"Well, I see my men have neglected to inform me you were running loose in my castle — once again." With a wicked laugh, he added, "But that is all well and good, because in the end I will be the chosen one to bring down the legendary Amáne of Teravinea. This time I'll take full advantage of my opportunity."

His female companion spoke up. "No, Galtero, don't. I can take care of her."

The legendary Amáne of Teravinea?

Ignoring the lady, Galtero's eyebrows raised as he moved toward me. "Oh? Do I detect a hint of uncertainty as to your identity? You still don't know who you are, do you?"

Revulsion rippled through me at the sound of his oily voice and the pleasure he took in recognizing my confusion.

"I know who I am, so you can wipe that smirk off your face."

I swallowed. *I know my name, but that's the extent of it.*

Struggling for a neutral expression, I hoped he didn't catch the part I left unsaid.

"You're lousy at lying," he said, his vile grin widening.

I pressed my lips together. Hatred burned in my heart.

His sword held vertical, he closed the space between us. I stepped back to keep the distance I needed for a strike with my glaive. We circled each other. I made the first move and feinted a lunge at him. His reflexes were good, even at his age.

Where's the woman?

I worked my way around to place her, once again, between Galtero and me.

How did that maneuver come so naturally?

I didn't know what she had in mind, but I certainly couldn't show her my back.

She cursed at Galtero. "I'm warning you. You must leave her to me!"

"Enough, Ravana, she's mine," Galtero barked at her. "Now, go. Follow through with our plans. I'll meet you once I finish her."

She didn't leave, but kept repositioning herself. I countered her movements as I dealt with Galtero.

Having the shorter weapon, he made smart use of the work tables and old storage jars in the kitchen, putting them between himself and my blade — to stay just out of my reach. He grabbed at anything not tied down and hurled it at me. I couldn't get close enough to throw a worthwhile shot.

A flying stool clipped my head. I let out a yelp and missed my footing.

"You're not as tough as the accounts claim you are, little girl." He said between breaths. He took the advantage and pressed toward me.

I shoved my shoulders back and rallied, parrying a series of his strikes. One after the other, but he still managed to push me back.

Galtero's next swing went wide. His control had lessened from the beginning of the fight. His breathing became labored. He stumbled. The black-caped beauty must have noticed as well. Galtero was losing his upper hand.

She called out to him in an angry voice, yet with a hint of fear. "Galtero, don't be a fool. Step aside and let me handle her."

Who is this lady that she can speak to her king like that?

But Galtero had his jaw set and his mouth pressed in a stubborn line. His resolve to kill me read clearly in his eyes. My intent to live eclipsed that.

Ravana cursed and rushed at us, her arms raised. She held no weapon.

Galtero and I now fought in the open. The lady danced for position, but I circled to keep him between us. He moved in close for an overhead shot. I brought my glaive horizontal and blocked his strike. Grunting, I pushed it up against him to trap his sword. Eshshah's strength still filled me. I let go of my right hand and reached behind me. With one swift move, I unsheathed my dagger from its scabbard at my back, brought it up under his rib cage and sank the blade into his black heart. Galtero's face twisted in shock and fear. Hot blood soaked my arm.

His eyes full of hatred stared into mine. I shivered. He grappled at the blade I still held embedded in his chest. His bony hands enclosed around mine and tightened with surprising strength.

BLACK CASTLE

Gurgling something incoherent, pink foam filled his mouth. His grip loosened. He slumped to the ground.

Before his body stopped twitching, Ravana shrieked, "Noooooo!"

She tore her eyes away from Galtero and shot me a ghastly look. My heart chilled. In the next breath, she raised her hand and made a throwing motion. A ball of fire blasted toward me. I leaped and batted it away with my glaive. As I looked on in shock, she hurled more fire balls.

She's the sorceress.

The lady showed no sign of slowing as she released the projectiles in rapid succession. I evaded and deflected them as she continued her barrage. The effects of my battles were wearing on me. I couldn't hold her much longer.

A searing pain exploded in my shoulder. The force spun me around and threw me to the ground. I screamed in pain. My glaive dropped and I grabbed my arm. Just as quickly, I released it. My hand had burned by just touching my injury. Eyes stinging from my smoldering flesh, I looked up to see the lady move toward me, a triumphant glow on her face. Like a spider stalking a fly caught in her web, she slowly glided closer.

I tried to get up, but could only manage a sitting position. My arm came up in a futile move to ward off her strike. Hovering above me, Ravana raised her hand to deal the death blow. She paused to gloat.

"Eshshah," I whispered. I felt her increased strength. Although my breathing became labored, my pain dulled enough for me to think.

The scale. I'd almost forgotten.

I kept my position on the floor. Praying the black-caped lady would revel in her triumph for one more breath, I reached in my sleeve to pull out Charna's black scale. Locking my gaze on the woman, and concentrating on her, I lifted the scale between us and quickly whispered, "Charna Yash-churka."

A black fog oozed from the scale. Increasing in density, it floated toward Ravana. Her eyes bulged. She froze, her hand still poised to throw her deadly fire. The lady's breath came out in rasping gasps. I watched in detached horror.

She must recognize the magic from Charna's scale.

The dark cloud encircled her head. It entered through her mouth, nose and ears. The sorceress took several steps backwards. Her eyes darted around the room as if seeing enemies surrounding her. The fireball in her hand brightened and then slowly faded out. Pressing her fists to the sides of her head, she let out a screech. The sound sent a chill up my spine. I pressed my lips together and watched as her terror increased. Batting the air, fighting off invisible demons, she fled out of the kitchen toward the courtyard.

"She's gone, Eshshah, thank you." I breathed in relief.

And thank you Charna Yash-churka I said to myself as I carefully placed his scale back in my sleeve.

I tried to catch my breath and take in the enormity of what I had just done. I'd sent several men to their ancestors, including the one called Galtero. Shaking my head, I dropped my shoulders.

Under my breath, I said, "May they all rest with their ancestors." A relief washed over me. My heart was moved, I had recognized I'd taken human lives.

Maybe I'm not the monster I thought myself to be.

"Let me sit here for just a moment, Eshshah, and then I'll head to the tunnel."

Before I could take in two more breaths, bootsteps echoed in the hallway. I forced myself up, wincing from the pain. Gritting my teeth, I grabbed my glaive and turned to face the new threat.

Black Castle

Thankfully, only one set of boots sounded in the corridor, heading toward the same door where Galtero and the lady had entered. I moved closer so at the least I could have the element of surprise. A drawn sword preceded my opponent into the room. I used the cross bars on my glaive to hook and draw it up and out of his hand.

My strength had waned. The attacker rushed fully into the room, still with a good grip on his sword. He turned to face me. My eyes went wide. I dropped my glaive and dipped into a painful curtsy.

"Your Majesty. I ... I'm so sorry. I didn't know ... I thought ..."

"Amáne!" King Ansel sheathed his sword. He pulled me up, drew me into his arms and buried his face in my neck. I stiffened as a multitude of emotions ripped through me.

The King of Teravinea had me pressed against his body. I inhaled sharply, but resisted the urge to push him away. I didn't want to insult this king who'd sacrificed his freedom for mine. What I found most unsettling was the intense heat that traveled through me as I stood enfolded in his embrace. Truthfully, his embrace comforted me. I almost didn't want him to let go.

A tangled mesh of memories swarmed through my head. I saw a crown and aristocratic ladies. But the images departed as quickly as they came.

Frustrated, I chewed on my lip and returned to the present.

How do I politely disengage myself?

He pulled back and took my face in his hands. His eyes went to my lips.

Is he going to kiss me?

My panic rose. Before I could act, he released his hold and stepped back. He held my hands while he gazed intensely into my eyes. The pain in his face confused me.

Bearing his grasp on my burnt hand, I cleared my throat. "I'm happy to see you safe as well, m'lord."

I tore my eyes from his piercing green ones and gently pulled my hands from his. As an excuse for my action, I tucked my hair back under my helmet, then turned my attention to inspect my sword belt as if I would find it in as much disarray as my emotions.

"My apologies. I didn't mean to alarm you," he said with a dip of his head.

His eyes scanned the room and took in the aftermath of my battles. Three guards lay in pools of blood. He threw me a shocked look as he moved toward the fourth body.

Kneeling beside it, he whispered. "Galtero."

I couldn't read his reaction regarding the fallen despot. Bowing my head to the young king, I said, "It was self defense, m'lord. I couldn't have taken him alive."

Approaching Galtero's body, I bent to retrieve my dagger that still stood buried in his chest. I shuddered, recalling his bloody hands grasping mine in his death throes. King Ansel gestured me away from the man, who looked just as evil in death. He extracted my blade, and after wiping it on Galtero's rich robe, he held it out to me, hilt first.

"You did a great deed. This man will no longer threaten Teravinea, or any surrounding lands, ever again."

I reached to take my dagger. The movement caused a shot of searing pain from the burn up to my shoulder. I yanked my arm back against my side with a gasp, leaving him holding the blade.

The compassion in his face made my heart quicken. He stood and ushered me away from the carnage to the far edge of the kitchen. After examining my arm, he took my other hand and turned it to survey the damage on my palm.

"How did you get these burns?"

"Galtero had a woman with him. A sorceress. The lady pulled cursed fireballs out of the air. I couldn't evade all she hurled at me."

His jaw tightened. "You're fortunate you had on a dragonscale breastplate. Your pauldron, your shoulder protector, took the brunt of the impact. But your upper arm didn't have any protection. They should have insisted you wore a rarebrace as well." He let out a sigh. "Let me wrap it until we can get you to Eshshah. She'll heal it for you."

"I'm fine, Your Majesty. We should leave immediately. The escape tunnel is behind you. My injuries are not important. They can wait."

He lifted his tunic and untucked his shirt. With my dagger still in his hand, he ripped through the fabric along the hem. "Between the two of us, I should be able to salvage enough strips to do a decent job."

Stubborn man.

"May I?" he said. Without waiting for my response, he tugged at the bottom of my shirt to find a section that wasn't soaked in blood.

King Ansel paused. "Are you hurt anywhere else? Is all this blood yours?"

I shook my head. "Most is not mine."

"I found a clean section. Hold still."

He worked around toward my back. Feeling awkward, I tensed up until he finished his task.

"There, now. This should be enough." The young king placed the strips on the worktable behind me, then took me by the waist and lifted me to sit on the table beside the cloths.

Heat rose in my face. "You really shouldn't be the one to wait on me, m'lord. It's not proper. I'm a commoner. I can wrap my arm myself."

His lips pressed together for a heartbeat.

Did I just insult him? Does he think I'm telling him what to do?

He picked my dagger up off the table and sheathed it in its scabbard at the small of my back. I inhaled his scent — a familiar scent. A fleeting recollection of images tortured me once again. I exhaled in vexation.

His eyes snapped to mine. "Are you all right?"

"Yes, I ... we've met before? I mean, before this place?"

"Your face is swollen. What happened?"

"You're not answering my question ... Your Majesty."

He stiffened and opened his mouth to say something. After a slight shake of his head, he asked, "You've met the Healer?"

"Yes. On your communication device."

"Then you know she's asked us to allow your recovery to come naturally. For reasons you don't understand. I choose to follow her instructions."

"You're the king. You don't have to take her instruction ... you don't have to take orders from anyone." My eyes narrowed. "Why the smirk?"

He shrugged a dismissal. "She knows what she's doing. There could be grave consequences if we don't heed her directives. Now, tell me what happened to your cheek. Are those puncture marks?"

King Ansel put his hand gently on the side of my face and drew closer to examine my snake bite. I leaned into his hand. Our eyes met. My heart beat wildly. The sound of his heart competed with mine.

Why would he also be affected by our closeness?

Ashamed of my inappropriate reaction, I inhaled and sat up straight. The king took a small step back. He bit his lip and dropped his eyes.

Black Castle

Swallowing the lump in my throat, I answered, "I was bitten by vipers. At least I thought they were vipers. Apparently they weren't, else why am I still alive?"

Without waiting for his response, I quashed my personal emotions and said with urgency, "Please, Your Majesty, I say again, my injuries can wait. We need to leave. Braonán will be waiting for me, for us, at the end of the tunnel on the north shore."

Ignoring my plea, he wrapped the strips of cloth around my arm. As he did so, I could hear the battle still raging outside. Dragons trumpeted their challenges. I was confident they would defeat what was left of Galtero's garrison.

King Ansel and I remained silent. I sat still and stiff on the table while he finished my arm and then my hand. I tried to keep my eyes lowered, but I couldn't stop myself from sneaking glances at him while he worked.

Who is this king and how does he know me? And more importantly, what am I thinking? I'm dangerously attracted to him. He is a king, Amáne ... but he's strangely alluring.

The young noble tended my injury with surprising skill. His task completed, I admired his handiwork. Without thinking, I said, "That'll probably leave a scar, don't you think?"

His head jerked back.

"What?" I said.

He blinked. "I just ... I've heard that before ... never mind. We'd best be going now."

King Ansel lifted me off the table, and handed me my glaive.

"By the way," he said, "I thought you'd like to know, Lia'ina and her group made it safely to the north shore. They were taken back to the inn."

"Thank you. That is good news."

He guided me toward the trapdoor of the tunnel with his hand low on my back — another gesture that sent my mind reeling with confusing images. A crown, again. Two ceramic dragons wrapped around a goblet. A stolen kiss.

Whom did I kiss?

I squeezed my eyes shut and bit my lip, but couldn't grab hold of the recollections.

The king bent down and pulled open the trapdoor. He motioned for me to enter the escape tunnel.

Before I took the first step, a thought came to me. Trying to hide my shock, I turned to King Ansel. "I beg your pardon, m'lord, but can I ask one more question?"

He nodded. "I can't promise I'll answer, but go ahead. And be quick."

"Er, was I ... that is, am I ..." My eyes wide, I blurted out, "Am I your mistress?"

The young king tried unsuccessfully to suppress a laugh. He shook his head and said, "Amáne, you were never my mistress." A mischievous glint came to his eyes, "But if you're willing, I wouldn't oppose."

My face went red. Biting back the urge to punch him, I spun around and descended the stairs into the dark tunnel.

CHAPTER TWENTY-EIGHT

The short flight of stairs ended at a dirt floor. Light coming down from the open trapdoor showed a narrow dark path before us. King Ansel would just barely be able to stand upright, and we'd have to walk single file. He waited until I reached the floor before he closed the trapdoor and secured the latch. Slivers of light seeped in around the edges of the hatch before being swallowed by the darkness.

I tensed. My heart raced. Closing my eyes, I inhaled and blew out a long exhale.

"Is something wrong?" the king said from close behind me.

"Please give me a minute." I inhaled slowly and exhaled again. "I'll be all right, it's just being confined down here ... I ..."

"You're claustrophobic?"

"Yes, I guess I am." I laughed nervously.

He rested his hands on my shoulders and pressed down firmly. Similar to what Avano had done for me before this mission, it created a calming effect. With his efforts and my breathing, I gained control.

"Thank you. I'm fine, now." I proceeded along the underground passage toward the north shore and safety. A sigh of relief escaped my lips.

"Amáne, if you don't mind my asking, what would make you think you were my mistress?" I heard amusement in his voice.

"First of all, I didn't *really* think I was your —" I blinked and started again, "Begging your pardon, my Lord King, no offense intended, but that's an inappropriate question and I'd prefer to drop the subject."

"As you wish."

I clenched my jaw. I also wished I knew what made me ask that question.

"We're on our way, Eshshah," I said out loud.

I heard a snicker behind me.

"What are you laughing at now ... if ... if you please, m'lord?" I stopped short and spun around on him, letting out a yelp as we collided. I stumbled backwards. He grabbed for me, and we both lost our balance. I exhaled an "oof" as I hit the ground, and another "oof" as he landed on top of me.

"Are you all right Amáne? I'm sorry, I didn't realize you were so close."

Thankful he couldn't see my blush, I stuttered to answer. The situation was so ludicrous, I giggled, prompting a burst of laughter from him.

He hesitated a bit longer than I thought proper, but finally lifted himself off and grappled in the dark to help me up.

I gathered my dignity and persevered with my query. "I'd like to know what you were snickering about."

"You spoke to Eshshah out loud."

I turned away from him and continued my trek down the tunnel. "I don't see the humor in that."

"It's just that it's not necessary. I don't expect you to know this."

"But I did know. I felt like talking to her out loud, that's all. But if it's that much of an issue ..." My nostrils flared. "I don't happen to know all of your rules and etiquette in your secret dragon society."

"My apology," he said in a low voice.

I almost regretted my outburst.

We stumbled along for a short while before I remembered my glaive had Eshshah's scales embedded. I whispered her name and a small flame grew on the end of the shaft, lighting the dark passage and alleviating my returning claustrophobia.

"Ah, that's much better," I said.

"I thought you'd never get around to that."

"You knew my glaive had Eshshah's scales?"

"Yes."

"Then why didn't you ask me to light it sooner?"

"I was about to, but I wanted you to be the one to remember."

"Begging your pardon, yet again, Your Majesty, you might be a royal and I might wish I didn't say this, but you can be annoying ... m'lord."

"So I've been told."

I could hear the smile in his voice. I huffed out a long breath realizing I'd become more at ease in his presence ... at least here, in the dark. I shouldn't be so comfortable with my disrespectful attitude.

Braonán had warned me it would be a long trek along the escape tunnel before we would arrive at the exit on the north shore. I knew we hadn't been down there long, but it seemed like hours we'd traveled in the dark, stifling passage. I was thankful for my glaive with Eshshah's fiery scales.

As we roved on in silence, my mind returned to my situation.

What kind of relationship did I have with this man ... this king? Why this overwhelming attraction? How well does he really know me?

I didn't want to admit it, but he had a charisma, a seductiveness about him that seemed so natural, not forced. More than likely he had this effect on all females.

Stop thinking of yourself as anyone out of the ordinary, Amáne. You are not worthy of his attentions.

But still the questions knocked about in my head.

What would it be like to kiss the handsome king who walked so closely behind me? How many women fawned over him, and how many had he wooed? My thoughts raged out of control. *Why did my obsession seem so wrong, and yet at the same time not wrong?*

Before I drove myself mad with my imaginings, I broke the silence with a topic I thought he could talk about. "If it pleases you, Sir King, would you tell me how you escaped and made it to the old kitchen?"

"Of course. I'm trying to piece it together, myself. Early this morning I'd anticipated your arrival, but Sovann, my dragon, hadn't heard anything. I worried, not knowing whether you'd made it in or not. It was quite a while before I heard you'd been captured."

"I'm not accustomed to this thought transference thing," I said. "I was a bit preoccupied myself, trying to stay alive. I contacted Eshshah as soon as I thought about it — once they threw me in a cell." I didn't mean for my response to have had so much heat.

"I understand, now," he said. "How did you manage to break free?"

"I thought this was your story."

"It appears at this point, the story is yours."

"Er ... alright, well, I guess my mission started badly because I'd been betrayed."

"Betrayed?"

"Yes, one of Lia'ina's tribe knew I was being smuggled into the castle in a crate. He gave me up. They threw irons on me and marched me into a cell."

How much should I tell him?

I shrugged and continued. "I'd just started to use Aperio's key when one of the guards came back. He seemed to remember me from ... before. The disgusting way he looked at me made my stomach turn. He let himself into my cell." I shuddered and found it difficult to continue.

"Amáne?"

"Hmm?"

"And then what? Did he hurt you?" Fear rang in his voice.

He took hold of my shoulder, stopped me and turned me to face him. "Did he hurt you?" he repeated.

"No. I managed to unlock my manacles and used them to knock him back, then I took his sword, and after a fight, I ran him through."

King Ansel huffed out a sigh of relief.

I squeezed his hand that still rested on my shoulder. "I'm fine," I said. Gently moving his hand off, I turned and continued down the tunnel while I told the rest of my story.

I related how I'd shown Lia'ina and her group the route to the escape tunnel, about Ramu'eno killing the traitor, finding my weapons and the guards' search for me as I hid in the storage closet.

Finishing my narrative I said, "I'm sure you heard the explosive results of the rest of my story."

I turned and walked backwards a few paces. "Now, I believe it's your story."

King Ansel took up his account. "As I mentioned, I feared something was amiss this morning. Now I understand it was because of your capture that they doubled my guard and moved me more frequently throughout the day."

He hesitated before he went on. "They had just unchained me from one location and were about to slap on another set of irons to transport me to a different site. That's when you ignited the first blast. I'll have to admit it took me by surprise, even though Sovann had warned me to expect it. The explosion proved a perfectly-timed distraction. You couldn't have chosen a more fitting instant."

I smiled.

He continued his tale. "I grabbed the closest guard's sword and had him dispatched before any of the others could make a move. The second man barely had his halberd at the ready when I finished him. It was hard to believe from seasoned soldiers, but the last two stood staring at me in shock. They went down without a fight.

"I headed toward where Avano waited, as planned, but at the first corridor, I heard the sound of boots around the corner. I had to duck into a dark alcove — narrowly missing getting caught.

"After they passed, there was no other option but to change direction and try the escape tunnel. I hoped you hadn't already latched it behind you, but I was prepared to break my way in. That's when I heard that unearthly wail. Then you screamed, and shortly after, I heard a horrible screech."

After several steps in silence, I said, "Your Majesty? King Ansel?"

I stopped, half-expecting him to bump into me again. Turning around, I could see him in the torchlight a number of paces behind me.

His voice full of emotion, he continued, "When I came around that door and saw you standing there ready to kill me, I was never more happy to see anyone in my life." He forced a smile. "I apologize for startling you. I didn't know what to expect. Just seeing you alive ..."

His sincere strength of feeling caught me by surprise. My eyes stung. I swiped at a tear that escaped down my cheek, hoping he didn't notice.

"I want to thank you for trading your freedom for mine, Sir King, although I'll never understand how the life of a commoner would be equal exchange for the life of a king. It makes no sense."

"What makes you so sure you're a commoner?"

"I might not know who I am, but deep down ... in my heart I know I was born without rank or title."

He shrugged.

"If you know otherwise, then please tell me," I said.

He shook his head. "I can't debate your birth."

A loud sigh of frustration forced its way from deep within my chest. I turned on my heels and continued on toward our destination.

I chewed at the inside of my cheek for a moment, then opened my mouth to voice one more query. Before I could utter a word, a low rumble, like a stampede of hoofed animals shook the ground. The rumble increased. The floor of the tunnel rocked violently. A rain of dirt sifted down from above.

The sound of my heartbeat thrashed in my ears. I groped for the walls — something to steady myself.

Buried alive. No!

I threw my arms around King Ansel. He pulled me close.

"Braonán told me there's another exit that lets out into the jungle," I said in a rush. "I don't know if we've already passed it. I haven't been paying attention."

"Sovann says it's ahead of us. We're close. Let's go."

"What's happening out there?"

"He says the volcano is erupting."

"Oh, so now we'll roast alive before we're buried alive?"

He shook his head, then grabbed my hand and pulled me toward the jungle exit. The tremors intensified, making our footing unsteady. Bouncing off the walls and stumbling, we searched for the escape shaft.

"It's here somewhere," King Ansel said.

My torchlight revealed an opening to our right. We turned, and in a few paces found the stairs we hoped would lead up to the exit. Reaching the overhead hatch, I prayed King Ansel had the strength necessary to open it. My energy had waned. I squeezed to the side of the stairwell, my back pressed to the wall for him to pass and access the trapdoor.

It was locked.

I started to pull Aperio's key out of my sleeve. He had already drawn his and whispered the dragon's name.

As he unlocked the hatch, another jolt shook the ground. My foot slipped. Grappling for something to hang on to, I found only air. With a cry, I tumbled back down the stairs. The tunnel collapsed around me.

I couldn't breathe. The dirt pressed in against my chest. It closed over my head. The sound of the king's shouting became muffled.

Panic won't save me. I will not let this be my end.

"Eshshah," I shouted in my head.

Her strength and comfort filled me. I worked my arm up through the dirt that covered me. Pushing with all I had, my hand emerged from my shallow grave. A firm grip closed around my wrist and pulled. Nearly out of breath, I struggled to claw my way out. My world spun. With a final yank from the king, my head broke the surface. I gasped in a lung full of air. King Ansel's terrified face hovered above.

He frantically dug around me. My shoulders and arms were freed. Locking his hands under my arms, I latched mine around the back of his neck. He must have called on his dragon's strength. With a powerful pull, the rest of my body emerged from my earthy prison. He fell backwards. I landed on top. My lungs exhaled with a huff.

I sputtered and coughed. The king held me tight and whispered my name.

My panic overcame any thought of rational behavior. I tightened my arms around him, and pressed my cheek against his.

"You're never so alive as when you're that close to death" — a quote I'd heard somewhere suddenly had great meaning.

We remained locked in each other's embrace for only a few breaths. I needed him for that brief moment. One final inhale, I closed my eyes and took control of my weakness.

Unlatching my arms, I pushed myself off of him. "King Ansel ... er ... thank you. We need to go."

The tremors continued. We scrambled to our feet, and charged up the stairs. King Ansel pushed on the unlocked hatch. It didn't budge. He put his shoulders to it and barely got it to move. I climbed to a higher step and hunched over, putting my back to the trapdoor.

"On the count of three, push," said the king.

Using my legs I shoved with all my strength.

"Come on, Sovann," he grunted.

Eshshah must have been in on that request, because I felt her increased strength.

"One more time, push."

With the dragons' help we felt the door move. Roots that had grown around the trapdoor ripped loose above us. Dirt spilled in along the edges. One more powerful effort and the ground overhead gave. The door flew open. We clambered out.

I fell to my hands and knees. Expecting to inhale fresh air, the rotten-egg smell of sulfur assaulted me. Stifling heat surrounded us. Hot winds whipped at our clothes.

"Get up, Amáne. We can't stay here." King Ansel had to shout over the howling wind and the approaching noise of trees igniting and falling. "Sovann says we're in the path of the lava flow. The dragons can't get in to us here through the thick jungle."

The king reached down and helped me to my feet.

"They've found a less dense area in that direction." He pointed ahead and to the right. "They're ripping out the foliage to clear it enough for Sovann to land. We have to go there."

Steadying myself, I looked over my shoulder. The jungle was thick, but through the vegetation I could see a red luminescence in the distant sky. The volcano. And another glow, closer. I turned and we bolted toward where the dragons worked.

Palm fronds and low branches lashed out at us. Thorny bushes caught on our clothes and exposed skin. The pain barely felt, we ran on.

Adding to the noise of the trees exploding in our wake, animals of every kind raced past. Monkeys screeched above as they swung from tree to tree, forest deer vocalized as they ran alongside of panthers — all in a panic to escape the approaching lava.

The jungle around us seemed to side against me. Roots caught my foot and I stumbled. Head over heels, I rolled down the embankment we'd kept to our right.

"Amáne!" King Ansel shouted.

Black Castle

The ground flew past me as I tumbled down the hill. I shot my hand out, grabbed onto a root and jerked to a stop. Pulling myself to my hands and knees, I looked up. My heart sank. I'd fallen too far. There would be no time to climb back up the steep incline before the area would be overtaken by the lava flow.

King Ansel began to pick his way down toward me.

"No, Ansel! I mean King Ansel. Go back. Please, save yourself."

I glanced behind me and scanned the bottom of the hill. A small stream reflected what little light filtered through the canopy. The rest of the way down didn't appear quite as steep as the slope from which I'd already fallen.

I shouted up at him. "Go back! I'll get to the stream and see if I can make my way to the dragons from there."

He continued down the embankment. "I'm coming, Amáne. Stay where you are."

Stubborn man.

The king slipped and skidded a short distance before regaining his footing. He cursed. Now he was as stuck as I.

I couldn't stay there and watch while he broke his neck trying to get to me. Clawing my way, I struggled to make it back up the hill.

This makes no sense. I'm not getting anywhere. And besides, I could no more catch his fall than he could pull me back to the top. We'd both break our necks or burst into flame, whichever comes first.

I shook my head, muttering under my breath, but kept trying.

Traversing a ways to his left, the young king drew his sword and hacked at a vine. Sheathing his blade, he worked his way back across to a tree straight up from my position. He tugged at the plant, pulling hand over hand. It loosened its hold from the jungle floor and he gathered it into a coil.

I nodded and smiled.

As clever as he is handsome.

Using the vine as a rope, he moved backwards down the steep hill, reaching me quickly. One hand holding the trailing plant, his other grabbed me and pulled me close. He kissed my forehead. Together, we stumbled the rest of the way down, using the vine until its length ran out. The last section of slope down to the stream was quite manageable.

The water felt good as we splashed into the middle of the shallow river. We took deep thirst-quenching drafts. I closed my eyes in relief as it went down my parched throat. We splashed the sweat and dirt off our faces, then turning left, we started upstream.

"Sovann says this leads further south from the area they've already cleared. They'll have to find a closer place for a landing zone."

"I told you to go on without me. Again, I'm responsible for endangering your life." A hitch in my voice betrayed my anguish.

He squeezed my hand.

"It would be faster if we didn't have to trudge through the water," I said.

"I've been looking, but haven't seen a path, yet. The brush is too thick on either side."

I bit back my frustration.

We struggled up through the river until we came to more level ground. A pathway revealed itself to our right — probably an animal track that led to the water's edge. Making our way to the trail, I had to stop to catch my breath.

Ash rained down upon us. Gasping for air, I looked to my left. Crackling sounds echoed close by. Sulfur and smoke burned my eyes.

"M'lord, we've run into the path of another lava flow. Do you think it can cross the river?"

"It would likely slow it, but I doubt the river can stop it."

My shoulders dropped. I moaned.

King Ansel stood before me. Grabbing my arms, he gently shook me and said between heavy breaths, "Amáne, pull yourself together. We will make it. It's not like you to give up."

He knows more about me than I know of myself.

I squeezed my eyes shut and rubbed my face with both hands.

His chest heaving, he bent over and grabbed his knees. "We'll make it."

He already said that. Is he trying to convince me or himself?

"We're racing the flow front," he said. "It's slow enough. We can outrun it." After several breaths, he added, "If only we had a vial of the Healer's potion."

"A vial?"

"Yes."

"Potion?"

"Yes," he said, losing patience.

"An awful tasting dark liquid?"

His head snapped up.

A bit taken aback at his angry look, I reached for a pouch that hung on my belt. Extracting a small vial of the Healer's concoction, I handed it to him. "Avano hooked it on my belt just before I left the inn. I'd forgotten about it."

King Ansel scowled at me then grabbed it from my hand. He pulled out the cork with his teeth and handed me the tiny glass container. "Drink it."

I tipped my head back and poured half the contents in my mouth. My face scrunched up at the horrible taste. I forced myself to swallow and then bent over in a coughing fit as I shoved the remainder at him.

"No, Amáne, you need —"

My eyes teared, my throat burned. "Take it," I growled.

The king shrugged, took the vial and downed the remainder. He must have been accustomed to the burn. He finished it without choking. Not even a cough.

I glared at him, an eyebrow cocked.

"You get used to it," he said.

I felt the warmth of the liquid as it traveled downward. A wave of alertness surged through me. I stood up straight, refreshed. "That's horrible stuff, but truthfully, it works."

"Remind me to give the Healer a big hug," he said smiling. "Now, let's go."

The king took my hand and we ran along the animal path with renewed strength and a restored perspective.

The lava gained on us as we neared where the dragons worked. I hesitated at the sound of crashing trees ahead of us. King Ansel urged me on. I picked up speed, realizing it was the sound of the dragons ripping at the vegetation to clear a spot for our rescue.

"We're nearly there," the king said. Relief sounded in his hoarse voice.

The heat followed us more closely. Fumes from the sulfur nearly overcame me. But I persevered. We reached the clearing. My stomach turned. I groaned. They hadn't cleared a large enough area for a dragon to land. Time had run out. The scorching heat singed the trees at the edge of the small opening in the jungle.

"We've made it," the young king said as he looked up to the dragons who hovered above the treetops.

"Are you mad, Ansel — King Ansel? Are we supposed to fly up to meet them?"

"You're not far from the truth. They're dropping an extraction line. Here it comes, look out."

Black Castle

I dodged as a rope fell from the air. Jerking my head in the king's direction, my eyes went wide. He swooped me up and placed his foot in one of the loops tied along the line. Shoving his hand through a higher loop, he held on. We rose into the air. I let out a squeal. A roar sounded behind us as a nearby tree burst into flames, toppling in our direction. The blaze seared my clothing as the tree crashed to the ground. Sparks flew high into the air.

I held tightly to King Ansel as Avano, on his grey dragon, Arai, lifted us out of the jungle.

"King Ansel, the rope!" I said.

Above us and out of reach, a red glow smoldered on the line.

"Avano, lift faster. Let Sovann get below us," the king shouted.

The sudden jerk strained the fraying line. I looked up in terror as the spark grew into a flame that crept up the rope.

Arai climbed to a height that sent my head reeling. The treetops receded below. Sovann's great wings pumped the air as he moved into position under us. He lifted smoothly, closing the distance. I stretched my foot out until it touched the saddle. He hovered closer, still.

"Grab the saddle bar, Amáne."

My heart raced as my hand clasped the bar at the front of the saddle. Trying to ignore the dizzying height at which we hovered, I slid my leg over the seat. Safely in, I reached to steady the line for the king to do the same.

At that instant, the rope burned through. King Ansel dropped. He grasped for the saddle, but missed. The king slipped past me. I screamed and grappled for him. My fingers closed around his wrist. I cringed in pain as I hung on, gripping the saddle bar with my other hand to keep myself from slipping off. My arms strained with his weight.

I can't hold him much longer.

Reaching with his free hand, King Ansel took hold of a metal ring attached to the side of the saddle. I let out a jagged sigh and sang a silent song of thanks. He hoisted himself up and latched on to the saddle bar.

Sovann spiraled up as the king pulled himself behind me onto the seat. He wrapped his arms around me. Leaning forward, he rested his head against the back of my neck.

Chapter Twenty-Nine

The view from high above the volcano's angry eruption was frighteningly awesome. As dawn lightened the sky in the east, the mountaintop glowed red in the north. A massive cloud of ash rose above its crater. Wide ribbons of lava oozed into the sea, creating spouts of steam. The mountain's south-facing bowl spilled over with more flows making their way toward the black castle. The thought overwhelmed me that moments ago we'd been trying to outrun the glowing mass of molten rock, and now from high above, I took in its ferocious beauty.

Adding to my wonderment, the ecstasy of flying filled my heart. Several dragon riders soared alongside of us, and one dragon without a rider. Eshshah. She flew wing-to-wing with the golden dragon upon which I rode with King Ansel.

"Thank you, Eshshah," I whispered.

She bobbed her head at me. Even from where I sat atop Sovann, I noted the sadness in her eyes. Poor dragon. She missed her rider.

"I'll help find her, Eshshah. I promise." I said silently.

My thoughts returned to my amnesia. This was the fourth day. The Healer said my memories should return within a few days.

What if they never did? What if my past never came back? Galtero had called me 'Amáne of Teravinea.' *Who am I?*

My throat closed. An involuntary sob shook my body. King Ansel leaned in to me. "Amáne, you're safe now, you'll be all right."

Afraid my voice would crack and give me away, I merely nodded.

Weariness overcame me. I was so utterly tired. Pain screamed out from every inch of my body. I couldn't wait to get back to the inn and tear off these scorched and bloodied clothes. I'd take a long hot soak and then sleep for a fortnight.

We hadn't flown long when we landed on a beach on the southeast coast. It remained untouched by the destruction that took place to the north. I glanced over my shoulder at King Ansel, a puzzled look on my face.

"I'm going to put you on Eshshah and send you back to the inn. The riders and I have to go back and make a sweep of the castle. Thanks to you, Galtero has met with his ancestors, but we hope to capture one or two of his advisors." He paused. "Or possibly the sorceress," he added softly.

My arm throbbed at the memory of that meeting.

"I'll see you at the inn by the evening meal," he said.

I blinked as an unexpected disappointment overcame me.

Could it be I'm reluctant to separate from this young king? What kind of fool am I?

Recovering my senses, I tempered my anxiety with the thrill of riding by myself. "I've never ridden alone. Does Eshshah agree to that?"

"She'd love to have you in her saddle."

"What about her rider? I wouldn't want to anger her."

His eyes darkened for only a heartbeat before he answered, "Her rider would want nothing more."

He led me to the beautiful red dragon. "First, please let her tend to your injuries."

I gasped. My eyes flew to the huge jaws hovering over me. Looking into her soft golden eyes, I exhaled and smiled. No danger or anything unfavorable reflected in them. At that moment I realized I'd come to fully trust the fiery red dragon. I tipped my head in acquiescence.

The king nodded at Eshshah. Having been around dragon riders these last few days, I'd learned to detect when they spoke to dragons in what they called thought transference.

Eshshah bent her great head down and pressed her nose to the soiled rags that wrapped my burnt arm. She exhaled a warm healing breath. I released a great sigh. King Ansel undid the wrap and Eshshah continued her treatment. The red dragon hummed a soothing sound as she healed my wound. Her heat coursed through my arm which burned uncomfortably hot before it turned to a tingling sensation and then to an itch. I couldn't pull my eyes away as my blackened flesh mended. The wound shrank, replaced by new unmarred skin. In a short space of time, not even a scar remained to remind me of my battle with the sorceress. Immediately after, Eshshah breathed her healing warmth into my hand.

The corners of my mouth turned up as I tested my arm, making circles with my elbow. "Thank you, Eshshah. You're amazing."

She tipped her head.

King Ansel smiled at my wonderment and said, "And look, no scar."

My eyebrows drew together. *Is he teasing me — referring to my earlier statement I'd made about a scar?*

He guided me to Eshshah's side. She crouched down with one foreleg pulled close. The king helped me up onto her leg and then hopped on behind me.

"Hold the ring here, and put this leg on the footpeg." His hand grazed my left leg. I inhaled at his touch.

"Good, now hoist yourself up into the seat. No, don't bend your knee. Swing your leg over behind the saddle."

I didn't tell him that's what I tried to do. My body wasn't listening to me.

As I sat stiffly, he buckled the straps that came out from the front of the saddle seat and secured over my thighs. Biting my lip, I closed my eyes and held my breath when he reached across my lap to buckle the far side.

"Thank you, Your Majesty. I could have done that one," I stuttered.

He tugged on and tested the rest of Eshshah's tack, then raised his face to mine. "Mora'ina will have a hot bath prepared for you when you arrive. You can soak for as long as you like."

My eyes went wide. "How did you — ?"

He gave me a warm smile, then patted my knee and leaped down off of Eshshah's leg.

"Just let Eshshah know when you're ready to take flight." He turned away and moved toward Sovann.

"Please be careful," I whispered.

Chapter Thirty

Neither the stifling weather of this tropical island of Orchila, nor the searing heat I'd experienced from the volcano could prevent me from insisting on steaming hot water for my soak. The heat of my bath water and the herbs Mora'ina added proved to be the catharsis I needed.

After a long while of reclining in the hot bath with eyes closed, I took in my first relaxed breath. Letting it out in a slow exhale, my attention turned to my healed arm. I ran my hand over the spot where my skin had been destroyed by the sorceress' burning missiles. It remained smooth and unmarked. Even the memory of the excruciating pain it had caused, began to fade.

Just above where my injury had been, the tattoo of a magnificent dragon stared back at me. Once again, I examined it closely, knowing it held a clue to my past. My eyes squeezed shut, but the marking triggered no memories. I lifted my right foot out of the water and scrutinized the other indelible design etched into my ankle. A different dragon. Not nearly as beautiful, this one looked misshapen, a mutant dragon. The significance of my markings escaped me. I closed my eyes again, refusing to lose the tranquility

I'd gained. Breathing in the relaxing aromas, I tried to clear my mind of all my unanswered questions.

I jolted when Mora'ina entered the bathing room. "Lady Amáne. Still breathe? Mora'ina worry. Long time in bath. Water too hot."

I laughed at her concern. "I'm fine, Mora'ina. Don't worry. I suppose it is time for me to get out, though. Thank you for keeping it hot for me."

She held out a soft towel for me to wrap in.

"Is the king back, yet?" I asked.

"No. Soon."

"Are they also searching for Eshshah's rider? King Ansel didn't mention her."

Mora'ina lowered her eyes then gestured toward a simple blue gown made of a light gauzy material. It lay on the bed along with clean undergarments. "Mora'ina help Amáne."

I let out a loud sigh. *Another unanswered question.*

"Thank you, Mora'ina. I don't need help dressing."

I scowled at the gown set out for me. "Must I wear this? Aren't there any other tights and shirts in my size?"

"Color beautiful for Amáne's eyes. Look like lady, not boy."

I bit back a groan but still rolled my eyes.

She hovered nearby while I donned the gown.

"Amáne take small food now," Mora'ina said as she moved a tray of fruit and cheese to a nearby table. "Big meal later."

Nodding, I sat at the table and shoved a piece of papaya in my mouth. After a few more bites of cheese, my eyes drooped with exhaustion.

The native girl eyed me with concern. "Amáne not can stay wake until big meal. No worry. You rest now. Okay to sleep in dress. Mora'ina wake Amáne later."

I hardly remembered her leading me to the large bed.

Chapter Thirty-One

I bolted upright and pulled my fist back to strike at my assailant. Mora'ina ducked. I checked my swing.

"Mora'ina! Forgive me. I ... I thought you were ... I dreamed I was ..."

I shook my head, pushing away the terror that eclipsed my mind. My eyes darted around the room filled with the shadows of the setting sun.

The native girl rested her hand on my arm and smiled. "Amáne no worry. No problem. So sorry Amáne scare. Big meal wait in dining hall. Get up. You go. First, Mora'ina make hair pretty."

I could have slept until the next day, but she was right in waking me. My stomach rumbled impatiently.

With experienced fingers, the Orchila woman quickly plaited and pinned up my hair. I held my tongue as she inspected my appearance and smoothed the creases from my gown. Satisfied with her efforts, she sent me on my way.

Trying to collect my nerves, I headed to the dining hall wondering how the king would receive me.

Stop with your foolish thoughts, Amáne.

Now that the quest had ended successfully, he would have no need for my services. I was merely a part of the operation for his escape. Possibly a nod of his head would be all I could hope to win. I knew I deserved no more.

Entering the dining hall, I surveyed the room. Filled with the dozen dragon riders of Teravinea and the small company of archers, the hall echoed with victorious voices. The mood was celebratory and sounded like double or triple their actual number. They sat at their tables, laughing and pouring drafts of ale. A few of them stood at my entrance, but seated themselves quickly after admonishing looks from their companions. Fighting down my confusion, I made my way between the tables.

The servers rushed around delivering steaming platters of roasted boar's head to each table. Following up with small pots of mustard. They carved the meat and distributed it on individual plates. My stomach growled again when the mouth-watering aromas drifted toward me. Sweeping the room, I sought the king. My heart skipped several beats.

He's not here.

Suppressing my disappointment, I found my usual spot. I nodded to Braonán across the table and slid in beside Avano.

"Amáne, pleased to see you've finally left your chambers to join us," he greeted.

"I had no choice. I could smell the food all the way from my quarters."

Avano smiled, put his arm around my shoulder and gave me a firm hug. "You did well. No. Better than well. Not only did you rescue the king, you rid us of Galtero. It was right that it be you who put an end to him, since you had such a past ..." His mouth clamped shut.

BLACK CASTLE

I leaned toward him, waiting for more. He shook his head and said, "Here, let me pour you a pint. A cask of DragonScale Ale arrived today. It's a special brew from Dorsal."

His eyebrows raised as if waiting for my reaction. Neither DragonScale Ale nor Dorsal sounded familiar. I offered a blank smile.

"I didn't rescue the king, Avano. It was he who found me. I would say he did all the saving. You can tell your stories to someone who might actually believe them."

Avano affected a hurt expression. I laughed.

In what I hoped sounded like a purely conversational tone, I said, "So, where is he? The king. Did he already eat? Will he be joining us in the dining hall? Oh, I suppose he wouldn't be dining in the common hall, would he? How silly of me —" I stopped when I saw the amusement on Avano's face and realized how I'd prattled on.

Fighting the heat rising in my cheeks, I turned, grabbed my tankard and took a deep pull.

"He should be joining us before long," Avano's lips twitched.

I swallowed the mouthful of ale and exhaled the breath I'd been holding.

A serving girl set a plate of meat and vegetables before me. I attacked it with fervor. As I savored the food, my attention was drawn to my ceramic plate. I studied the pattern of concentric circles pressed into the clay. It had been thrown on a potter's wheel.

How do I know this?

I stared at my dish. The food grew faint, as if it no longer existed. Just the empty ceramic plate. It rippled and began to spin around and around. Long graceful fingers, wet with clay, pressed into the plate. My gaze rose from the forming piece. A woman sat at a potter's wheel, her apron spattered with clay. She spoke with me, and we laughed as she worked.

Mother.

My eyes took in the small shed in which I stood. A workroom, with pottery in various stages of completion sitting on shelves around the room.

"I'm thirsty, Amáne. I have to get this order finished. The ship leaves in two weeks."

I nodded at my mother and ran across the yard to our cottage. I stepped into the simple kitchen to fetch her a cup of water.

I'm not alone. My mother waits for me.

"Amáne?" Avano pulled me out of my reverie, his hand rested on mine.

Elated, I turned to him "I remember, Avano. I live in a small cottage. Just my mother and myself. She's a potter. Do you know her?"

His mouth twitched.

"The riders are inviting you to join them in a toast."

Taking ahold of his sleeve, I shook his arm. "Did you hear me, Avano? I said I remember. I think my memories are coming back. My mother is a potter. She makes ceramic wares and ships them throughout Teravinea." I brightened at my success. Hope lifted me.

"She *was* a potter, Amáne," he said softly.

"Was? Then what does she do now? I can't recall that part."

Avano's eyebrows drew together. His hand squeezed mine. "Amáne, she rests with her ancestors."

As if someone had punched me full in the stomach, I couldn't breathe. My lower lip trembled. The noise in the room couldn't drown out the panic that screamed in my head.

Black Castle

I'm an orphan. An orphan and a commoner. The lowest ...

My jaw tightened as I glared at him. "You're wrong. I know you are."

His lips pressed into a flat line. He shook his head. "I'm sorry, Amáne."

The din in the hall converged into words. The soldiers shouted, "A toast to Amáne."

Attempting a smile, I lifted my tankard. I glanced around the room with glazed eyes. The rowdy group of the king's men, both dragon riders and soldiers; the hall flowing with food and drink; the fine quarters I'd been allowed.

None of this would be for me once I return to Teravinea. I'll be alone. Darkness swirled around me.

The riders cheers echoed as if in the distance.

Someone slipped in next to me on the bench. My stomach twisted.

He's here and I missed his entrance.

I turned to my left. My eyes went wide. "Lia'ina. I'm happy to see you."

She wrapped me in a warm hug. I returned it just as sincerely. Pulling back, I caught her sending a worried look over my shoulder to Avano. She gave him a quick nod back.

Taking my hands, she pressed them to her forehead. "Amáne look beautiful. Lia'ina leave for village, now. Gather tribe and go live in peace in Valley of Ancient Dragons. Please to visit one day. Lia'ina wish healing to Amáne."

She placed her hand on my cheek. Her eyes glistened. Biting her lip, she nodded once, then rose and rushed out of the room before I could respond.

I watched in perplexed silence as she left.

Another who knew me before. How does a native from this remote island share a history with me?

My eyes stung. My throat hurt. Clenching my teeth, I turned on Avano. "What was that all about? Some secret looks letting her know 'the poor girl' is still missing her mind? Do you have to act like I'm not here? That I don't understand what's going on?" A searing flash of anger seized me.

Avano held his hands up as if in surrender. "Amáne," he said.

As I looked daggers at him, the noisy room became silent. The occupants in the hall stood like ripples in a pond, and bent their arms in the dragon salute. Barely managing to quell my fury, I rose from the bench and joined the men in saluting King Ansel's entry.

"As you were," he said as he strode through the room.

My anger cooled. I slowly took my seat as my heart lodged in my throat. I'd only known the king through the trials of our escape. Both of us disheveled, dirty and tense. Quite the opposite in his entrance, he radiated royalty. He wore a shirt of midnight blue with billowing sleeves under a golden dragonscale breastplate; black tights and high boots; his long dark hair pulled back in a queue with several leather thongs tied at intervals. A light circlet of gold rested on his head. I barely managed to close my gaping mouth.

The king scanned the room before his eyes rested on me. A slight smile formed on his lips. He headed in my direction.

Breathe, Amáne. Take a breath.

King Ansel's smile sent my stomach on a wild ride. It shone a light on my dark mood, fading it into the background, at least for the moment. He folded his tall frame into the bench across the table from me and reached out his hand for mine. Pulling it toward his lips, he pressed a kiss on it. The room felt quite unbearably hot.

He didn't let go of my hand. His eyes drew me in. "You look ravishing, Amáne."

Stunned at his compliment, my mind flashed to a memory of someone saying the same thing to me. I'd stood on a staircase and looked down at the person. The face at whom I stared remained in shadow.

Another memory. But can I trust it?

Pulling myself back to the present, I said, "Thank you, Your Majesty. And you are looking ..." *Magnificent, enticing, seductive.* "... very nice, yourself." I shifted uncomfortably, hoping whatever dragon magic he had didn't include reading minds.

My anxiety increased as he, without further conversation, continued to hold my gaze. I gently pulled my hand back and cleared my throat, "So, your search was fruitful, Sir King?"

"Most of Galtero's troops were wiped out. We found no one of importance."

Nodding slowly, I swirled my knife around my plate. That meant they hadn't encountered the sorceress.

I wanted to find out if they also searched for Eshshah's rider, but I didn't feel it was my place to raise the question at that moment. All the time I'd spent with King Ansel and I never asked him about her. No mention had been made of her whereabouts or if she'd been captured by Galtero — only that she was missing. It seemed odd that everyone had ceased talking about the lady. Because of me, they all tended to guard their speech.

Nothing came to mind that I thought a worthwhile topic to discuss. Our recent escape wasn't a subject I wanted to bring up, so I ate in silence. Throughout the meal I could feel King Ansel's gaze upon me. He'd turn to a dragon rider and exchange a few words, or laugh with a soldier, but I noted his laughter didn't reach his eyes. Always, he drew his attention back to me.

My focus remained on my plate. I welcomed the numbness embracing me and found it easy to reject the cheerful mood that filled the dining hall. The revelry gave support to my desire for reclusion. Add to that, King Ansel's nearness sent my mind hallucinating a multitude of impossible scenarios — some of which sent heat rising up to my face.

You are truly mad, Amáne. Have you always been this foolish? You are a commoner. Royalty does not associate with someone of your station.

Dark confusion whirled in my head. I knew my home lay somewhere in Teravinea. I was sure to be returned to where I belonged, but what then?

What if my memories never come back?

Dizzy with fear, I clutched the edge of the table until my knuckles turned white. A jagged sigh slipped from my lips.

The king's eyebrows drew together. A shadow crossed his green eyes. "Amáne, I can see how hard this is for you. You'll recover. I know you will. Trust me, there is good reason we can't help with your memories. There's a delicate balance with ... certain connections ..." he pressed his lips together and shook his head. "You must be patient. Don't push it."

Hot anger, radiated from the pit of my stomach and rose to a crescendo that I struggled to control. I leaned across the table toward the king. Tightening my hand around his wrist, I whispered between clenched teeth, each word distinctly pronounced, "King Ansel, you have no right to tell me —"

His jaw tightened and his head jerked back.

Black Castle

My eyes went wide. I let go of his wrist and bit my lip. Standing abruptly, I stepped back over the bench. "Your Majesty, I beg your forgiveness. If you all would please excuse me." My voice quavered.

The king's face fell in disappointment. "It's all right, Amáne. There's no need for you to leave."

My heart constricted at his expression. He looked like a lost boy.

A lump grew in my throat. *Oh yes, there's great need. I need to get out of here before I scream — or start smashing plates. Or, before the king calls for my arrest.*

I tipped my head, curtsied and said with surprising control, "I bid you a good evening."

Trying for a dignified exit, I spun around, straightened my back and walked steadily through the door. Once I reached a safe distance, where no one in the hall could see me, I bolted out into the night.

I've insulted the king. Why didn't he have me clapped in irons? He just let me walk away.

My hands closed into fists. I fought the urge to cry out — to beg for someone to tell me my past. Everyone treated me with such caution, catching themselves from saying too much, as if I would shatter.

What is it they're trying to protect me from? Or, maybe they're trying to protect something else ... from me?

The Healer had let something slip. She mentioned I had some kind of connection, or link that could be damaged if my memories were forced. King Ansel just admitted the same.

A connection to what, or to whom?

Tears streaked my face. I pressed my fists into my temples. My head throbbed. But I kept running.

I rushed on blindly, and wasn't surprised my escape took me to where Eshshah lay. She lifted her head from her front legs and watched me approach. I gave her a dragon salute and stopped directly in front of her. The red dragon lowered her eyes to my level. I took hold of her fangs and brought her nose to my forehead.

Why does this feel so natural?

"Eshshah, I wish you could talk to me. I know you could give me the answers I need. If I'm not healed by tomorrow, please, I'd like to try again."

Eshshah breathed her warm aromatic breath on me. I inhaled her spicy scent. It washed over me and eased my pain.

"But, whether I'm healed or not, I vow to you I'll help you find your rider. Once we do and she is returned to you, I only ask that you not forget me. You need to know that you've become a part of my life. I hope that doesn't break any rules. Perhaps your rider would let me take one last ride with both of you before we go our separate ways."

Eshshah hummed a calming tune. Letting go of her fangs, I stepped back, but wasn't ready to leave her presence. She was my comfort. I needed whatever I could get.

I moved to a spot behind her front leg and leaned my back against her, then slid to the ground. Eshshah curled her head around. One golden eye fixed on me. My tears fell freely before I succumbed to a restless sleep. Even with her extraordinary healing powers, Eshshah couldn't completely relieve my misery.

When I awoke, the stars were bright in the sky. Dawn still remained several hours away. Rising to my feet, I said farewell to

Eshshah and headed back to the inn. I wondered why no one had come out looking for me and then realized they'd probably been in communication with Eshshah. They knew I was safe. It occurred to me there was no privacy among dragon riders.

Chapter Thirty-two

I admonished myself for sleeping late. Already my chambers filled with the morning light. Sitting up, I squeezed my eyes shut and searched my mind. Nothing. No new recollections. I remained the same Amáne as yesterday, with no past beyond the last few days.

My lip quivered.

Enough of this weakness, Amáne.

A burning determination filled me. I stuck my chin out. Maybe my memories would never return. But I had to continue with the rest of my life. Decisions had to be made. I knew I had useful skills, however acquired. I'll make good use of them. If I couldn't hope for my recovery, then I would be hope for someone else. Eshshah's rider would be my first task. She needed to be found. I'd vowed to Eshshah I would help.

I keep my promises.

A light knock sounded on my door and Mora'ina let herself in. She had a long piece of fabric draped over her arm.

Not another gown.

"Happy morning, Amáne," she said cheerfully. "Meal in dining hall. Get up. You dress." She spread the fabric on the bed.

BLACK CASTLE

Just as I thought, a flowing gown, this one in green, made out of the same gauzy fabric as the other.

I rolled my eyes. "Mora'ina, are there no tights and shirts that I could wear instead? I don't want to wear a gown."

"Amáne want look like boy?"

"Yes. I do. I'm more comfortable that way."

"This most comfortable. Amáne wear."

"If it's so comfortable, why aren't you wearing one?" I indicated her cropped top. Colorful fabric that wrapped her breasts and left her midriff bare. And the just-as-colorful skirt that rested low on her hips.

She brightened. "Amáne want wear kikoi like Mora'ina? Tradition island dress. Make look very pretty. I bring."

"No. No, thank you. I'll wear the gown."

I promised myself the first chance I got, I'd search the inn for tights and a shirt that would fit me.

Mora'ina smiled, then helped me don the gown.

"Mora'ina fix hair."

"No, I don't need my hair done. I'll wear it down." I said it with a bit more fervor than I intended. She shrugged and nodded.

"Then, Amáne, ready. Go to eat."

"Mora'ina, could I ask you to bring some food here? I need some time alone so I can think."

She dipped her head and turned toward the door. A short time later she returned with a plate of thin-sliced meat, some soft white cheese and a piece of flat bread. I nodded in appreciation as she put it on the table. I didn't miss the look of pity in her eyes before she left. I sighed.

I reflected on my situation as I spread some cheese on a piece of bread and topped it with a slice of meat. Some riders mentioned they would be leaving for Teravinea today. No one had mentioned taking me with them. Surely that would be the plan. After all, Teravinea, was my home. I knew at least that much. Maybe I should inform them I wouldn't be going back just yet, but would go at a much later date. I could negotiate transport aboard a ship. There should be plenty that sailed south from Orchila's port.

What would be my excuse to stay on the island?

You're scared, Amáne. I huffed at the only reason why I would stay.

Orchila was all I knew. Teravinea held the unknown.

Nothing is working for me.

I closed my eyes and chewed at my lower lip. Indecision circled me like dark waters, pulling me under.

I should go to Teravinea to face whatever awaited me. But what about Eshshah's rider? I needed to speak with someone who could tell me about the missing lady and when they planned to search for her. I'll count myself in with the search party, whether they want me or not.

A weight lifted from my chest. I had a plan.

Pushing my empty plate away, I rose from my seat. I took a deep breath, smoothed my hair back and headed out the door. I'd go straight to the king and ask him, regardless of protocol. Perhaps I should have asked someone to make an appointment for an audience with him. Too late.

My decision is made.

The worse that could happen would be I'd be escorted out. Or, there was still the possibility he'd have me arrested for my insolent behavior the night before.

My heart beat louder and faster as I approached his quarters. I wiped my sweaty palms on my dress. My breath caught in my throat. The truth came to me. My anxiety had nothing to do with the impromptu meeting I'd decided upon.

You've fallen in love with him, Amáne. There, I've said it. And that is sheer madness.

The discussion I planned to have with the king wasn't about me or whatever feelings I had for him. My attraction to him was irrelevant at this point. Eshshah suffered. I couldn't allow that after all she'd done for me.

I promised. I will do this for her. The king need never know of my feelings.

Stopping several paces before his door, I tried to calm the tremors that coursed through my body. This meeting was necessary. I took several more deep breaths.

Moving a few steps closer, I raised my trembling hand to knock and overheard a conversation on the other side.

"I just want her back, Avano." Anguish filled the king's voice. It tugged at my heart.

"I know, Your Majesty. We all wish the same."

I stood frozen. The door swung open. I jumped. Avano ran straight into me. I bounced off his chest. He grabbed my arm to prevent my fall.

"I'm sorry, Avano. I wasn't ... that is, please don't think I was trying to listen in. Er ... I hoped for an audience with the king. I ..."

King Ansel rushed up behind Avano. "Is everything all right?"

I smoothed my dress and inhaled.

His eyes sought mine. I noted at first a hopeful glint reflected in them, but was quickly replaced by shadow.

"Yes, Your Majesty." I curtsied. He frowned. I stepped back in retreat, then looked over my shoulder. All I could see of Avano was his back as he headed down the corridor. I swallowed the panic rising in my throat, wishing he hadn't abandoned me.

"I didn't mean to disturb you m'lord. I can certainly return when you aren't occupied."

"No, please come in. Don't curtsy to me any more."

I blinked at his abruptness.

He has every right to be angry with me.

"If it pleases you, m'lord."

"It does."

He held his hand out for mine. Puzzled, I placed my hand in his and tried to ignore its strength, its warmth. Treating me as if I were a lady and not a commoner, he led me to a couch, and gestured for me to be seated.

King Ansel stared at me for a few moments, seemingly lost in thought, or maybe trying to collect himself. He smiled warmly and sat down with me.

"To what do I owe the pleasure of your visit?"

He surely bounces from curtness to politeness.

"Firstly, I need to offer my apology for my rude behavior last night."

"No apology necessary."

I nodded then pulled back my shoulders and with an official tone, I said, "King Ansel, I've come to offer you my services."

He raised an eyebrow. The corners of his mouth lifted in a roguish smile. "Just what services do you propose to offer, Amáne?" He leaned in.

My eyes widened. My mouth moved, but nothing came out. I couldn't stop the blush that rose in my face.

He's enjoying my discomfort.

My embarrassment transformed to anger. I wondered what the penalty would be for striking a king.

Black Castle

As I looked into his dancing green eyes, I realized I couldn't be the one to put a shadow on his amusement. I exhaled and decided to forbear my anger for his respite. He must be suffering greatly.

I cleared my throat. "Your Majesty, my services to help find the lady." My words came out slowly and distinctly.

"The lady?" His head tilted.

"Yes. Eshshah's rider, your friend, your mistress, your —"

"My wife."

Instantly, the air was sucked out of the room. My chest tightened. I struggled to take a breath.

"Oh." I scooted a bit further from him, and hoped it didn't appear too obvious. My hands clutched the fabric of my gown. When my breath resumed, it came in short, shallow pants.

I have to find a way to excuse myself without offending him.

Jumping to my feet, my voice broke as I said, "I'll do whatever you ask of me to help you find her."

Why am I offering to torture myself?

My eyes stung as I curtsied, forgetting his request against the gesture. I backed away.

As I turned for the door, he said, "You don't have to leave ... Amáne. Your presence is a comfort to me."

I let out a quick breath. My steps halted.

I'm a comfort to him? Now I find it's his wife that he is lamenting and somehow I comfort him? What kind of role did I play in his life?

Panic rose, my throat tightened as he moved close behind me and placed his hand on my shoulder. He turned me gently. I lifted my face. King Ansel's passionate eyes drew me in.

Stepping closer, he whispered, "May I kiss you?"

I gasped as I struggled between anger that he would betray his wife and my desire to kiss him, ashamed of myself for even considering it.

I dropped my eyes. "Excuse me m'lord, I must go ... I have to go ... I need to go ... I ..."

Trembling, I spun around and rushed away from him, toward the door.

I heard his heavy sigh. "I want you to know," he said quietly, "I won't give up on you — I'll wait for you. I promise."

My hand hovered above the door latch. I blinked. A violent storm assailed my memories. My pulse throbbed in my ears. Without turning, I said, "What did you just say?"

"I said, 'I'll wait for you. I promise.'" With a note of fear in his voice, he added, "But, I ... I'm afraid I've said too much."

I'll wait for you?

Episodes of my life illuminated around me — my linking with the beautiful red dragon.

"Eshshah?" I said silently. "Speak to me, please."

"Amáne?" Her tentative voice floated gently in my thoughts. "Are you back?"

"Yes, Eshshah ... I'm here. Now I understand ... it was our linking that was in danger ... the reason everyone had such concern."

"Yes."

Her relief and love flooded my heart.

I clenched my fists and squeezed my eyes shut as more scenes of my past played before me — rescuing Ansel in the dungeons of Castle Teravinea; the battle for the throne ... our wedding. Pain erupted in my head. I bit my lower lip.

I wanted to rush to Eshshah. I wanted to rush to Ansel. Instead, I stood as if paralyzed.

"Amáne, I long to see you, but I can feel King Ansel needs you more at this moment."

I took in a great calming breath, then slowly turned and met Ansel's troubled eyes. "You said those words to me a long time ago ... Ansel."

He dipped his head in a slow nod, prompting me to continue.

"I know who I am." A smile grew on my lips.

He took a step toward me, but stopped. His eyes flashed with concern, eyebrows raised in hope.

"I'm the missing rider — your wife. I'm back. All of me. I'm here."

My heart beat so loud, I could barely hear his response.

"Amáne, my love."

I threw myself at Ansel, wrapped my arms around him and pressed up against his warm body. My whole being shook with sobs. He buried his face in the crook of my neck. We clung to each other.

Ansel pulled back. His fingers entwined in my hair as he held my face, studying my eyes, my nose, my lips. He covered my mouth with his.

A wild surge of heat flooded through me. Our kiss ignited the room.

Breathing hard, he said, "Let's go home."

I raised an eyebrow and said, "Let's take up where we left off ... first."

Acknowledgments

When I set out to write my story, I thought the series would be a trilogy. The characters, however, called for more. They had me wrapped around their fingers, insisting I wasn't done. I had to listen to them. So I continued the story. And truthfully, I can't see that it is finished yet. Too many more adventures left to be had.

Of course, as I've said before, the support and encouragement I received kept me writing. My family, including my daughters, April and Alanna gave me valuable input with grammar as well as flow. Their daughters, Rio, Mila and Kira are my muses. My husband, Lloyd, my sister, Doreen and my son-in-law, Jason are my biggest fans. Again, Scott Saunders adjusted and improved upon my fight scenes, Michael Clark shared his creative suggestions, thoughts and ideas, the dancers of Linda Armstrong's School of Highland dance were a few of my beta readers, and Forrest Vess offered his design input for my cover (and nodded graciously as I babbled on about the various issues of the writing process). My Tuesday Meet-and-Critique group, including but not limited to Alison, Candace, Craig, Donna and Jeanne raised the bar high to improve my writing skills.

Thanks to all of you who continued to ask when this fourth book was going to be done. I finally finished it for you!

THE AMÁNE OF TERAVINEA SERIES:

THE CHOSEN ONE

∾

THE PROPHECY

∾

THE CROWN

∾

BLACK CASTLE

D. María Trimble lives in Carlsbad, California with her husband. Her days are spent as a graphic artist at a local company. She has been a student of dragonology from a very young age.

Made in the USA
Monee, IL
01 June 2022